OUR

JOHN BLACKBURN was born in 1923 in the village of Corbridge, England, the second son of a clergyman. Blackburn attended Haileybury College near London beginning in 1937, but his education was interrupted by the onset of World War II; the shadow of the war, and that of Nazi Germany, would later play a role in many of his works. He served as a radio officer during the war in the Mercantile Marine from 1942 to 1945, and resumed his education afterwards at Durham University, earning his bachelor's degree in 1949. Blackburn taught for several years after that, first in London and then in Berlin, and married Joan Mary Clift in 1950. Returning to London in 1952, he took over the management of Red Lion Books.

It was there that Blackburn began writing, and the immediate success in 1958 of his first novel, *A Scent of New-Mown Hay*, led him to take up a career as a writer full time. He and his wife also maintained an antiquarian bookstore, a secondary career that would inform some of Blackburn's work, including the bibliomystery *Blue Octavo* (1963). *A Scent of New-Mown Hay* typified the approach that would come to characterize Blackburn's twenty-eight novels, which defied easy categorization in their unique and compelling mixture of the genres of science fiction, horror, mystery, and thriller. Many of Blackburn's best novels came in the late 1960s and early 1970s, with a string of successes that included the classics *A Ring of Roses* (1965), *Children of the Night* (1966), *Nothing but the Night* (1968; adapted for a 1973 film starring Christopher Lee and Peter Cushing), *Devil Daddy* (1972) and *Our Lady of Pain* (1974). Somewhat unusually for a popular horror writer, Blackburn's novels were not only successful with the reading public but also won widespread critical acclaim: the *Times Literary Supplement* declared him 'today's master of horror' and compared him with the Grimm Brothers, while the *Penguin Encyclopedia of Horror and the Supernatural* regarded him as 'certainly the best British novelist in his field' and the *St James Guide to Crime & Mystery Writers* called him 'one of England's best practicing novelists in the tradition of the thriller novel'.

By the time Blackburn published his final novel in 1985, much of his work was already out of print, an inexplicable neglect that continued until Valancourt began republishing his novels in 2013. John Blackburn died in 1993.

By John Blackburn

*A Scent of New-Mown Hay* (1958)★
*A Sour Apple Tree* (1958)
*Broken Boy* (1959)★
*Dead Man Running* (1960)
*The Gaunt Woman* (1962)
*Blue Octavo* (1963)★
*Colonel Bogus* (1964)
*The Winds of Midnight* (1964)
*A Ring of Roses* (1965)★
*Children of the Night* (1966)★
*The Flame and the Wind* (1967)★
*Nothing but the Night* (1968)★
*The Young Man from Lima* (1968)
*Bury Him Darkly* (1969)★
*Blow the House Down* (1970)
*The Household Traitors* (1971)★
*Devil Daddy* (1972)★
*For Fear of Little Men* (1972)
*Deep Among the Dead Men* (1973)
*Our Lady of Pain* (1974)★
*Mister Brown's Bodies* (1975)
*The Face of the Lion* (1976)★
*The Cyclops Goblet* (1977)★
*Dead Man's Handle* (1978)
*The Sins of the Father* (1979)
*A Beastly Business* (1982)★
*The Book of the Dead* (1984)
*The Bad Penny* (1985)★

★ Available or forthcoming from Valancourt Books

# OUR LADY OF PAIN

JOHN BLACKBURN

*with a new introduction by*
GREG GBUR

VALANCOURT BOOKS

*Our Lady of Pain* by John Blackburn
First published London: Jonathan Cape, 1974
First Valancourt Books edition 2014

Published by Valancourt Books, Richmond, Virginia
*Publisher & Editor*: James D. Jenkins
*20th Century Series Editor*: Simon Stern, University of Toronto
http://www.valancourtbooks.com

All Valancourt Books publications are printed on acid free paper
that meets all ANSI standards for archival quality paper.

ISBN 978-1-941147-23-8 (*trade paperback*)

Set in Dante MT 10.5/12.7
Cover by M. S. Corley

# INTRODUCTION

On the evening of December 29, 1610, in the Castle Csejthe in what was then the Kingdom of Hungary, a decades-long nightmare ended – and an undying legend began. Responding to persistent rumors about the sadistic habits of the Countess Elizabeth Báthory, a group of nobles and armed guards descended on the Castle unexpectedly. They were led by György Thurzó, then the Prime Minister of Hungary and ironically the steward of the Widow Báthory and her children.

What they discovered at the castle was worse than they could have possibly imagined. Right within the entryway, they came upon a young girl who had been savagely beaten to death. Going further inside, they found two more girls who had been stabbed and beaten. From there, the sounds of screaming led them to four servants of the Countess in the process of torturing yet another young woman. The Countess was not with them, but they found her in her private chambers soon afterwards. She was indignant at the intrusion and apparently indifferent to the horrors she and her servants had wrought.

In the investigations that followed, Countess Báthory was exposed as one of the worst serial killers of all time. Though estimates vary, at least thirty girls – and perhaps hundreds – were tortured and murdered by Báthory and her select circle of assistants between the years 1585 and 1610. The crimes even long preceded the death of her husband Ferenc Nádasdy in 1604, and he must have turned a blind eye to her actions.

The crimes were a national scandal and were quickly covered up by the aristocracy. The story nevertheless spread, however, and grew more elaborate, ironically fueled by the lack of secrecy surrounding it. The Countess's actions were incomprehensible to people of that time, and the tales told provided their own explanations. It was said that the Countess, fifty years old when apprehended, was bathing in the blood of her victims in an attempt to regain or preserve her own youthful vitality. Elizabeth Báthory became known as the Blood Countess,[1] a moniker that has persisted to this day.

The Countess's story – truth and falsehoods alike – has been featured in fiction for more than a century. An early notable story is 'Eternal Youth, 1611', written by Leopold von Sacher-Masoch in 1874. Sacher-Masoch's writings, which often featured women dominating over submissive men, led to the term 'masochism' being coined after his name. In recent years, Elizabeth Báthory has experienced a revival in fiction, being featured as both protagonist and supporting character in a variety of novels, typically as a vampire. She is mentioned, for instance, in the 2010 novel *Abraham Lincoln: Vampire Hunter* by Seth Grahame-Smith as a key figure in the history of vampirism. She is also the main villainess in the 'official sequel' to Bram Stoker's *Dracula*, the 2010 novel *Dracula the Un-Dead* written by Dacre Stoker (Bram's great grand-nephew) and Ian Holt. In 2014, Linda Lafferty's novel *House of Bathory* was published, describing the curse of Báthory haunting people in modern times.

However, long before her current macabre fame, Elizabeth Báthory was featured in the 1974 novel *Our Lady of Pain* by John Blackburn who, as you will read, had quite a different take on the character. His novel is one of the earliest appearances of Báthory in English literature, and one of the most striking. Blackburn's novel is as much a mystery novel as a horror novel, and it succeeds on both fronts.

His tendency to combine and thwart genres made John Blackburn (1923-1993) an extremely popular and well-regarded author during his long and prolific career. Before taking up writing, he drifted through a variety of jobs: lorry driver, teacher, schoolmaster, radio officer in the Merchant Marine. It was in his last regular position, as the director of Red Lion Books in London, that he took up writing. His first novel, *A*

---

[1] My description draws heavily on the details in Kimberly Craft's 2009 book *Infamous Lady: The True Story of Countess Erzsébet Báthory*, which seems to be the only detailed biography of the Countess written in English.

*Scent of New-Mown Hay*, was an instant success when it was released in 1958, and Blackburn stepped down from Red Lion to pursue writing full time. He would write a total of 28 novels, the last being *The Bad Penny* in 1985.

*Our Lady of Pain* was written arguably at the highest point of Blackburn's career, during a handful of years in which he produced truly unique horror fiction. Among these works was his 1968 novel *Nothing but the Night*,[1] which was turned into a 1973 movie produced by, and starring, the veteran horror film actor Christopher Lee. In fact, it appears that Lee inspired *Our Lady of Pain*; it is said that Lee suggested the legend of Báthory as a story idea.[2] Blackburn, in turn, dedicated the novel to Lee. Curiously, I have not been able to find any direct confirmation that Lee suggested the idea, but it is certainly plausible. Christopher Lee had close connections with the Hammer Films production company, and one of Hammer's films was Countess Dracula, released in 1971, about none other than Báthory.

*Our Lady of Pain* is not only one of Blackburn's best novels, but also one of his darkest. It features a genuinely flawed protagonist, journalist Harry Clay, who is desperate to break a big story. When he serendipitously overhears a professional criminal talking about a mysterious heist, he is willing to do just about anything – including breaking the law himself – to learn more. The investigation leads to a plague of suicides, in which the perpetrators of the heist have killed themselves to escape being haunted by their worst fears. Further exploration shows that a sadistic doctor named Paul Trenton is somehow involved, and Trenton himself is treating the famous and temperamental actress Dame Susan Vallance. Vallance is slated to star in a new stage production only days away – about the life of Elizabeth Báthory. As the opening of 'Our Lady of Pain' draws near, Clay races to understand the deadly secret connecting everything – and risks his own life and sanity in the process.

[1] Also available from Valancourt Books.
[2] This bit of trivia is mentioned in numerous places on the internet, such as Wikipedia, but I have found no citations to confirm it.

*Our Lady of Pain* follows a similar trajectory to many of Blackburn's horror novels. In many of his stories, including his first, *A Scent of New-Mown Hay*, a mysterious malady afflicts the population, and a few brave and intelligent people must race to find the source and a cure. However, most of Blackburn's other novels feature larger-than-life stock characters, notably the cunning British Intelligence agent General Charles Kirk and the brilliant bacteriologist Sir Marcus Levin. In *Our Lady of Pain*, however, these heroes are absent, and it is primarily the desperate Harry Clay who must save the day. This increases the tension of the story considerably, as compared to Blackburn's other works. The only stock character who makes an appearance is Harry Clay's boss, the odious newspaper editor John Forest, who had previously served as a nuisance in the aforementioned *A Scent of New-Mown Hay* as well as *Nothing but the Night*.

We have noted that the story of Elizabeth Báthory has been warped and exaggerated as the centuries have passed. For perhaps obvious reasons, Blackburn primarily uses the fictional aspects of Countess Báthory's life in the novel, and adds his own new embellishments to it. This should not be taken to mean that Blackburn did not research his subject, however; he was a well-read author who ran his own antiquarian book store on the side and incorporated many ideas from history, science, and current events into his writing. *Our Lady of Pain* is perhaps the best illustration of this, as it employs many literary and historical references. The most obvious of these is the repeated mention of 'Room one hundred and one', a nod to the torture room in George Orwell's classic *1984*, which is said to contain each subject's worst fear. There is a brief mention of 'something nasty in the woodshed', which is a reference to a recurring joke in the 1932 novel *Cold Comfort Farm* by Stella Gibbons, which parodies the period novels of the Brontë sisters, among others. Blackburn mentions a few odd books in the novel, including *The Book of Were-Wolves*, written in 1865 by the prolific author and Anglican priest Sabine Baring-Gould. Later, when Harry Clay attempts to explain the suicidal delusions of the professional cons, he mentions the 'Mad Dancers' of the Middle Ages, people who found themselves uncontrollably compelled to dance, even to collapse. Also known as 'St Vitus's Dance', this mysterious ailment erupted a number of times in Europe, notably in Aachen, Germany in 1374 and in Strasbourg, Germany in 1518. It has been suggested (and is mentioned in the novel) that this dance may have been caused by ergotism, a fungal infection of rye that can cause hallucinations. A mass ergot poisoning in the town of Pont-Saint-Esprit in southern France in 1951 affected 250 people, leading to 50 people being institutionalized and 5 deaths.

The center of the story, however, is always Elizabeth Báthory. After the discoveries at her castle, her servants were put on trial for their crimes; three were brutally executed, while the fourth was sentenced to life in prison. Báthory herself was never subjected to a trial; the involvement of a noblewoman in such horrors was too scandalous to be publicly exposed. Instead, the Countess was imprisoned in her home castle, literally bricked up in a small set of rooms, with only small openings allowing for the provision of food and ventilation. She lived like this for another four years, and was finally found dead in 1614. It is not difficult to imagine such a malevolent spirit surviving through the ages and eager to seek revenge; John Blackburn's *Our Lady of Pain* provides a remarkable and chilling imagining of such an event.

Greg Gbur
April 25, 2014

GREG GBUR is an associate professor of physics and optical science at the University of North Carolina at Charlotte. He writes the long-running blog 'Skulls in the Stars', which discusses classic horror fiction, physics and the history of science, as well as the curious intersections between the three topics. His science writing has recently been featured in 'The Best Science Writing Online 2012,' published by Scientific American. He has previously introduced four other John Blackburn titles for Valancourt Books.

For Christopher Lee, with gratitude

We play with light loves in the portal,
And wince and relent and refrain;
Loves die, and we know thee immortal,
Our Lady of Pain.

A. C. SWINBURNE

# Preface

'THE GHOUL OF THE GLASGOW GORBALS. Not a bad headline, Harry; quite catchy in fact.' Fat John Forest, news editor of the *Daily Globe*, craned over the current edition spread out on his desk. 'And it's followed by a nice vivid write-up. I'm moderately pleased with you.'

'Thanks John.' Harry Clay was very tired and his eyes ached behind the contact lenses which he'd worn since his last pair of spectacles had been broken while he was covering a Women's Lib demonstration for world peace. But the compliments revived him slightly, because Forest was a hard task-master and even *moderately* pleased was high praise from his lips. Reporters who roused the fat man's displeasure were liable to end up on the dole, or be relegated to one of Global Enterprises' two local papers: the *Fulham Clarion*, and the *South-West London Guardian and Advertiser.* 'Those Glasgow killings were pretty sensational, so I thought a sensational treatment was in order.'

'You thought correctly, dear boy.' Forest nodded like a vast china Buddha while he studied the article. ' "Jamie Macdonald, the beast who terrorized an entire city, is caged at last . . . Once again, women can walk the streets in safety, and children play without fear of assault." Yes, just the kind of pretentious tosh our readers love; bless their empty little bird brains.

'They've given your picture a good spread too, Harry; very flattering indeed.' He leaned over and studied his subordinate, who was an untidy young man dressed in a sports jacket and a roll top sweater. 'Over-flattering, and you'll have to smarten yourself up for this evening. I presume my secretary has told you about the assignment.'

'She gave me a pass to the Pegasus Theatre and said you wanted me to review a production of Shaw's *Saint Joan*.' Harry's elation dwindled. 'I thought there'd been a mistake at first, John. Hell's bells, I've only just got back from Glasgow, and I'm not a drama-critic. I haven't been to a theatre for years or read any Shaw since I was at school.'

'Then a bit of culture will improve your mind, son, and it's a question of "Needs must when the Devil drives," I'm sorry to say. Half the staff have been laid low by this blasted 'flu epidemic that's on the rampage and there's no one else available.' Forest had had a late and heavy lunch and he stifled a belch. 'Your ignorance of the subject should prove no drawback because I certainly do not require a scholarly analysis of the show from you. After all, we are a family paper.' He stressed the term cynically, meaning that the *Globe* catered for readers who were unable to absorb a column of print unless it was liberally spaced with pictures and sub-headings.

'However, though we normally fill our pages with crime, sport, gossip about the Royal Family and attacks on whatever government happens to be in power, tonight is a special occasion.' A fin-like hand drew a theatre programme from the desk drawer. 'After a long absence, Dame Susan Vallance returns to the footlights in the role of Saint Joan, and, as everyone knows, Miss Vallance is one of the great ladies of the English stage. Surely you agree that a representative of the *Globe* should be present?

'Yes, a very great lady is Susan Vallance, though not a popular one.' Harry had remained silent and Forest continued, flicking through the programme as he spoke. 'The public consider her conceited and as for her Thespian colleagues . . .' He paused and pushed the programme across the desk. 'They hate her guts.'

'I can guess why.' Harry looked at a photograph of the actress. Though middle-aged, Miss Vallance was still an extremely beautiful woman, but there was a hint of domineering arrogance in her expression that explained Forest's statements. 'One of the "I'm right, you're wrong, and that's that" brigade. I bet she's a bitch to work with.'

'Shall we be charitable and say that she's a perfectionist, Harry.' Forest heaved himself up from his seat and paced the office floor. '*La belle Vallance* sets a high standard for herself and demands it from others. She bullies writers, producers and technicians and gives the supporting cast hell if they're not up to scratch. Hardly the best way to win friends and a lot of people would be delighted if she flopped this evening.

'Not that she will flop, of course.' Like many stout men Forest could move as smoothly as a cat and he seemed to glide across the carpet as though castors were fitted to his feet. 'Dame Susan may be a tartar who enjoys humiliating leading men and reducing young actresses to tears, but she's a born trouper and you'll see an impeccable performance. More's the pity, because our readers are always regaled by the fall of unpopular public figures.

'So you needn't worry too much about the actual play, my boy. Just give a competent layman's opinion and concentrate on the atmosphere and social side. Bright lights and glittering tiaras, the arrival of Lord Broadacres and his lovely daughter, Lady Pamela. You know the kind of guff.'

'I should do after four years on this rag, John, but there's something a bit odd here.' Harry had been reading a biographical sketch beneath the photograph. 'Apparently Miss Vallance's last show was *The Merchant of Venice* which closed eleven months back. An extremely long time for her to have rested.'

'Ill health, Harry. She was a wonderful Portia and *The Merchant* had been playing to full houses, but she collapsed in her dressing room before a matinée and couldn't go on any more. Minor cardiac trouble aggravated by overwork and nervous strain was the official explanation, but a little bird told me what strained her nerves.' The fat man halted by the window and stared thoughtfully over Fleet Street. 'Apparently Madam had been more demanding than usual throughout the production and one of the sufferers struck a blow for freedom. Not a nice blow to give a lady – not nice for the lady to know that she inspires so much hatred.

'We couldn't print anything unfortunately. My informant was not an actual witness and he heard the story from Dame Susan's dresser who later retracted her statement.'

'I'd like to hear the story though, John.' Harry had scant

interest in the theatre, but an intense curiosity about human behaviour. 'You mean she was physically assaulted?'

'In a sense, though nothing as vulgar as a slap on the kisser or a punch in the guts took place. The injury was self-inflicted and Miss Vallance cut herself. Only superficially as it happens, but she might have been partially blinded and the shock would certainly rock anybody with a groggy heart.

'No, not a nice thing to have done – not nice at all.' Forest turned from the window and grimaced. 'Someone planted a razor-blade in her stick of eye shadow.'

'That's that then.' Ten hours had passed, the curtain had fallen on *Saint Joan* long ago and Harry had finished dictating his copy to the news desk.

'A theatrical occasion which will long be remembered.' He replaced the telephone, frowned at his shorthand notes and lit a cigarette. '. . . Large, glittering assembly graced by the presence of royalty . . . arrival of the textile heiress, the former Ellen van Grossman, with her fifth husband . . . Clive Baxter, the racing motorist, whose left arm is still in plaster . . . tense anticipation as the audience waited for the rise of the curtain.' Harry crossed to a sideboard in his flat and poured himself a whisky. There had been tension at the theatre all right and Forest's belief that Miss Vallance was an unpopular figure was clearly correct. The walls of the foyer were studded with her photographs and he'd seen several people eyeing them with obvious dislike.

'. . . Those two knights of the theatre, Sir Roland Lampton and Sir William (Billy) Backhouse looking bronzed and fit after their triumphant tour of Australia . . .' So far – so good. Harry squirted soda into his glass. That part of the story had been easy to write, but the review itself had given him a deal of trouble.

'. . . Lavish production . . . delightful sets . . . convincing study of the Dauphin by Peter Stanning . . . added force to the trial scene . . . the kind of performance one expects from Dame Susan Vallance . . .' Harry sipped at his drink with only a slight twinge of anxiety. For better or worse the job was done and there was no point in worrying, because the paper was going to bed. Lavish production was O.K.; the budget guaranteed that, and the sets had been delightful. He'd chatted to Ray Jacques, the *Daily Blast's* critic, who'd seen a preview of the scenery, and Ray had been in raptures.

But what about the play and the acting? Was Stanning convincing as the Dauphin? Had the producer given the trial scene added force? Was Miss Vallance's performance up to standard? It would be interesting to see what the other papers had to say, Harry thought, because he hadn't a clue. Shortly before the curtain was due to rise he'd slipped out into the street for a breath of air; he'd seen Doc Trenton leaving the stage door, and Forest's instructions went to the winds.

For Paul Trenton's character had interested Harry since the day the man had walked into the *Globe* building to sell his life story, and it had obsessed him before the story was finished. The sad story of a surgeon struck off the register for negligence. Harry had ghosted this tale of woe, and at first its narrator had raised his sympathies, because on the surface Trenton was a pathetic person. Before the two actions for damages and the Medical Council's hearing he had been a portly man of forty-five, but tribulation had aged him and he looked a good sixty. A gaunt, unhappy old man had aroused Harry's pity, but the emotion did not last. It suddenly turned to loathing during their final interview when Trenton made one tiny slip and Harry realized the truth. Paul Trenton had not been negligent and he was not an object of compassion. His acts had been deliberate and he was that mercifully rare phenomenon: a completely evil human being.

No more slips were made however and Trenton still looked thin and haunted when the *Globe* paid him and he went off to live abroad. But that was two years ago and he didn't look haunted outside the theatre. It took Harry a moment to recognize the plump, well-dressed figure strolling nonchalantly away from the Pegasus, and when he did recognize him all thoughts of *Saint Joan* vanished and his obsession returned.

Doc Trenton was back in London and he was on the up and up again. The Doc's resurrection could provide a story and Harry followed him as automatically as iron is drawn towards a magnet.

When he'd ghosted the Trenton memoirs Harry had worn a beard and thick-rimmed glasses and there was little chance that he would be recognized. Shadowing Trenton was not a difficult task, though it proved a fruitless one and gave him no clue to the man's present way of life or circle of acquaintants. Trenton had bought an evening paper which he read over two pink gins in a nearby public house. Trenton had walked to Soho, pausing before the windows of several pornographic bookshops on his way, and eaten a long and exotic meal in a Greek restaurant. Trenton had left the restaurant, browsed before more windows and then suddenly hailed a passing taxi – the only taxi in sight. Trenton was driven away and Harry had gone home to fabricate his copy for the *Globe*. Harry was becoming just a trifle anxious.

Though there was no need to be, he reassured himself. His comments on the play were as ambiguous as possible. 'Interesting study . . . added force . . . kind of performance one expects.' Who could challenge such statements? Certainly the *Globe*'s readers wouldn't. Probably they'd enjoy the glittering assembly, shake their heads disapprovingly over the textile heiress's change of husband and be relieved to know that Sir Roland and Sir Billy were bronzed and fit. But they'd hardly glance at the actual review and, unless the theatre had caught fire, nobody would know that he'd deserted his post.

All the same it would be comforting to talk to somebody who had actually seen the show. He'd telephoned Ray Jacques, who was still out and his wife had promised to get him to ring back later. But there'd been no return call and when the time came for the paper to go to bed he'd had to dictate his fictitious notice.

That was probably Jacques now. The telephone rang and he laid down his glass and hurried to answer it. 'Harry Clay here. Is that you, Ray?'

'No, Sweetie, it is John. Dear old John Forest.' The editor's voice sounded friendly, but he slurred his words as though he had been drinking heavily, which was not uncommon. 'I've read your copy, Harry, and I'm delighted that Miss Vallance was her usual scintillating self. Did you enjoy your evening?'

'It was just a job.' Harry remembered the dejection he felt when Trenton's taxi disappeared round a bend. 'I hope you're satisfied with my treatment.'

'I am proud to know that we have such an imaginative and creative writer on the staff, Harry, but I must point out that we are not publishers of fiction.' There was nothing friendly in Forest's tone now, and Harry realized he was cold sober and extremely angry. 'You may recall my saying that people would be pleased if Miss Vallance flopped, and I have just spoken to somebody who actually saw the play. One of the glittering assembly you mentioned in your article, which I have been unable to stop – which is being printed at this very moment.' He paused to draw breath.

'For your information, the woman did flop and damn badly. She muffed several short lines, had to be prompted through the longer speeches and all her former magic was lacking. Susan Vallance was like a half-dead zombie, and that's not all.

'They slow-handclapped the poor cow when she took a curtain call and she lost her temper. Marched up to the edge of the stage and abused the audience – more or less told 'em they were a load of bloody morons, and your review will make us the laughing stock of Fleet Street.' Forest was bellowing down the line and Harry moved the receiver away from his ear.

'All our rivals will have headlines crucifying Susan Vallance, and you . . . you . . .' There was another pause while he considered Harry's fate. 'You're going to be nailed up on a cross of your own, my boy.'

# Chapter 1

'Naturally I share your hopes, but I am still far from sure that they are justified. There may be nothing except a material treasure. Gold, coin of the realm and precious stones; quite trivial things.' The speaker was sitting in the front passenger-seat of a parked Rolls-Royce Silver Cloud. 'Sir Arthur's motivation could have been equally uninteresting from our point of view. Childish superstition is the popular theory, because this part of the country was notorious for its witch trials during the period in question. Another notion is that it was a simple matter of teratology like the Glamis horror.

'Teratology is the study of monsters and monstrous births, madam. A subject which has long fascinated me.' His companion had questioned him and the man grinned slightly and looked down at a heavy, vellum-bound volume laid open on his lap. The book was old and stained and musty and its appearance clashed with his freshly-tailored suit, his neat brown hair, and white, well-manicured hands. A prosperous and benevolent man on the surface, who might have been a senior director of an old-established company. But only on the surface, and he wasn't a company director and he wasn't benevolent. The mind behind his florid face was racked with bitterness and his prosperity was of recent origin and might not last long. That possibility did not worry him unduly however. He liked good food and clothes and all creature comforts, but he could do without them. His other needs were more compelling and his name was Paul Trenton, once a member of the Royal College of Surgeons.

'All the same, it is clear that pressures were put upon Sir Arthur Holtby from very high quarters; certainly by the earl and the bishop.' The book was in manuscript and Trenton took out his glasses to decipher the faded handwriting. ' "His Grace and His Lordship are wise and honourable men and their arguments have convinced me that I must yield to their demands. Satan's presence has been revealed in this house, great evil troubles the land and there is only one possible source. The treasure which my beloved wife did leave me on her deathbed is accursed, and my mind is resolved. Preparations for its concealment have been made, and may God have mercy on my soul." ' The car was parked in a lay-by on the crest of a little hill. The windscreen faced the Essex coast and the woman at Trenton's side studied a cluster of buildings near the sea while she listened to his reading.

' "Tomorrow is the feast of the Blessed Saint Michael, Scourge of Demons, and a fitting day for the deed to be done. That which I find fair and others foul shall be encased in leather and sealed with a lock. Beauty and immense riches will lie hidden in darkness, so that no common man may look upon them." ' Trenton raised his eyes and followed her inspection of the buildings. A rambling Tudor manor-house with cottages and stables and a tree-lined drive. 'Yes, encased in leather, that fits in with your belief, and the last seven words are most significant.'

'Quite so, Doctor. No common man might look at those hidden things, but members of the Holtby family might, if they dared to break an oath.' A breeze was blowing in from the sea and the woman wound up her window and smoothed back a lock of hair. 'We know that in 1643 Sir Arthur started a tradition which was observed for almost two hundred years. On his seventh birthday each male heir was told the location of the hiding-place and what it contained. He was then made to swear the following affidavit. "Should I, through greed, malice or wanton curiosity seek to profit from this knowledge, may the fires of hell burn me eternally."

'Poor little boys. It's no wonder that the treasure was left untouched till Gilbert Holtby plucked up courage in 1828. A brave man, Gilbert, though poverty is a keen spur and a spendthrift wife gave him his courage.' She waited while a lorry rumbled past and then quoted from memory. ' "Hetty's extravagances have well-nigh beggared me and her ceaseless demands are costing me my reason. The Jews screech and batter at my door and servants clamour for pay.

' "But why should I suffer when the means of salvation are to hand? There is nothing to fear from Sir Arthur's treasure trove for flesh cannot defy time. But metal and gem stones can survive and my debts are more pressing than the superstitious vow I made in my youth. Before the week has passed, I and my mason, Allan Fenwick, will have entered the hiding-place." '

'Here's the reference that follows.' Trenton had turned to the end of the book, which was a diary compiled by members of the Holtby family for six generations. ' "I remain in good bodily health, but poor Fenwick's hideous death throes trouble my conscience and the sight I saw after I removed the visor will haunt me for the rest of my life. Everything we took from that hell-hole has been returned and the breach resealed by my own hands. From this day the tradition is ended and no son of mine will be told what lies hidden." '

'That's the last entry, though Gilbert Holtby lived for several years after writing it.' Trenton closed the book. 'Your late uncle by marriage had no other papers that might have helped us?'

'Not that I know of, Doctor. My uncle was a bankrupt and he died in a state lunatic-asylum. After his death, the public receiver allowed me to select one small personal memento and naturally I chose the diary.' She paused and lit a cigarette. 'The house was sold to a property company who intend to build bungalows on the site and we have little time to waste. Demolition work is due to start on the first of next month.'

'Very little time.' Trenton took a copy of the *Daily Globe* from the glove-tray and checked the date. The paper was open at the centre page and an article stated that Dame Susan Vallance was fully recovered from the indisposition which caused her to leave the *Saint Joan* production and would shortly be appearing in a new play. 'Exactly a fortnight, so we shall have to move fast.'

'That is why I wanted to show you the lie of the land. As you can see, the house is quite deserted and you will be able to assure your associates that they will not be disturbed.'

'Associates?' Trenton's expression registered surprise. 'You mean to involve other people at this stage?'

'Naturally, because neither of us has the strength or skill to hack our way through brickwork. But you are a man of parts, my friend.' The woman gave the ghost of a smile that had no warmth or humour. 'A doctor of medicine, something of an antiquary, also a criminal. A small time drug-pusher, before I picked you out of the gutter. Surely you have acquaintances who would be prepared to join forces with us.'

'It's possible.' Trenton ignored her insult and stared thoughtfully at the buildings. 'Yes, I do know one or two people who would be suitable, but though the house is empty there is so little time. It might take several weeks to search such a huge barn of a place.'

'An hour or two should be sufficient, Doctor.' The woman smiled again and pulled at her cigarette. 'As I told you, my uncle, David Carslake, was only a relation by marriage who inherited the house from my mother's sister, and he had no qualms about treasure hunting. Before his mental breakdown last year he measured out the interior of the building and found a discrepancy in the dimensions. That prompted him to cut a little hole in a wall.

'I visited Uncle David in his madhouse now and again. He had delusions that the nurses intended to torture him and usually was quite incoherent. But on my last visit, shortly before his persecution-mania came to a head and he hanged himself on a dressing-gown cord, he was fairly lucid. He told me about the hole he had drilled and what he saw when he shone a torch through it. All your associates will have to do is go through the house till they find a spyhole in one of the interior walls and that's that.'

'What did your uncle see?' Trenton rubbed his hands together which he often did when he was excited. 'Did he tell you in detail?'

'I think he saw something that was to drive him out of his mind later, but at the time it didn't interest him. Money was David Carslake's only goal and in the asylum he kept repeating the biblical phrase, "Jewels of silver and jewels of gold." The material treasure will be ample payment for your burglar friends.' As though the topic had ceased to interest her she took the newspaper from him and frowned at a photograph of Susan Vallance. 'How lovely that face used to be. How sad that the muscles grow slack and the skin wrinkles.'

'That happens to all of us, but stop keeping me in suspense.' Trenton gripped her arm. 'For Christ's sake go on and tell me what else your uncle saw behind the wall.'

'For Christ's sake! A strange expression from you, Doctor, and you disappoint me. You are also hurting me.' She pulled her arm away from him. 'My uncle was concentrating on financial gain and he had no eyes for anything else. But surely you have enough imagination to guess what he saw and failed to recognize.

'Consider the reference in the diary. "That which I find comely and others foul shall be hooded like a hawk . . . Flesh cannot defy time . . . Poor Fenwick's hideous death throes." Also consider that it is a mere three months since my uncle killed himself and Sir Arthur Holtby hid his treasure in the seventeenth century.' She laid aside the paper, switched on the car engine and then stared him in the face. 'If you're still a Doubting Thomas shall we go to the house now and look for that hole ourselves?'

'No thank you. Foolhardiness is not one of my failings and I have work to do, so please take me back to London.' Though the weather was cool Trenton's forehead had suddenly become damp with sweat. 'What you imply is scientifically impossible. It goes against the very laws of nature, but if you're right . . . if a miracle did take place . . .'

'You and I are going to profit from that miracle.' The woman eased the car into the road. 'Surely it's obvious that when Arthur Holtby concealed those jewels of silver and jewels of gold which my uncle saw, he knew they were well guarded. Isn't it also apparent that after . . .' She made a mental calculation. 'Three hundred and forty-four years the thing that guards them is still alive and kicking?'

# Chapter 2

'TYCOON MURDERED OUTSIDE SAVOY . . . M.P. ON RAPE CHARGE . . . TANKER HOLOCAUST . . .' Harry Clay sat in the Feathers saloon bar glumly studying the *Globe*'s headlines which had all been composed by other men. His own contribution to the news was tucked away in the *South-West London Guardian and Advertiser* and consisted of a caption reading LAUGHTER FOR HIS LORDSHIP, followed by a brief report that a bishop had cracked a joke while opening a primary school.

Laughter for his lordship! Harry's gloom increased and he recalled the last story he had written for the *Globe*. The Glasgow murders and his photograph on the front page. HARRY CLAY REVEALS ALL.

But that was nearly six months ago and his glory was in the past. Though John Forest had not been able to carry out the crucifixion threat literally, he'd done the next best thing and civic correspondent of the *Advertiser* was not an exhilarating position. Harry's life was now devoted to bishops and mayors opening schools, mayoresses gushing at flower-shows, and aldermen pontificating about the rates. There was small prospect of release either, because he was under contract to Global Enterprises and Forest had got him by the short hairs.

'Forget about looking for a job with another firm, my boy,' the fat man had said with a cigar jerking between his lips. 'You've let me down and I haven't got a forgiving nature. You'll stay with the *Advertiser*; I've told the editor to give you all the dullest assignments he can think of, and there's only one thing that'll put you back in my good graces.' He removed the cigar and pointed it at Harry like a pistol. 'Stumble on to a real story, follow it up on your own and write me a scoop. Till then, or till the day your contract expires, it'll be COUNCILLOR DOGSBODY IN FINE FETTLE for you.'

RETURN OF WEST END STAR. Harry looked at the *Globe*

again and an announcement that Susan Vallance would soon
be appearing in a new play which had been specially written
for her. 'Damn Miss Vallance – damn *Saint Joan*, and damn
Doc Trenton,' he muttered to himself, taking a pull at his pint
of bitter beer. It was just before noon; he rarely drank in the
morning, but he had popped into the Feathers for old times'
sake, because he had often used the pub when he was on the
*Globe* and it was an interesting one. A rendezvous of thieves
and con-men and tarts, where information could be gleaned at
times. He'd heard a lot of strange stories in the Feathers and
seen some strange transactions take place there. But it was too
early for the regulars to arrive, and apart from the barmaid and
one elderly man reading a sporting paper at the counter, the
room was empty.

Yes, damn Paul Trenton, whatever he's up to, Harry repeated
silently. Shadowing the Doc had been a fruitless labour which
cost him his job, but his obsession remained, and a friend in the
C.I.D. had told him something about the man's recent movements. Apparently Trenton had returned to England some
weeks before Harry saw him outside the theatre and he was
broke on arrival. Police interest was aroused because he was
often seen in the company of known criminals, but the asso-
ciations did not last long. The ex-surgeon suddenly vanished
from the underworld scene and both his cronies and the police
lost track of him.

'That bleedin' Doc started it all.' For a moment Harry
thought he was hearing himself speak, and then he glanced at
the partition at his side. There was a knot-hole in the woodwork and the voice came from the adjoining public bar. 'I got
the horrors, Jim, and they're driving me out of my ruddy mind.
Started in the dark when I was in bed, but it's worse now. Any
dim light brings 'em on and I can't take much more. On the
way here I crossed the road under a subway and there they
were behind me. It was so bad that I had to stuff a handkerchief
into my mouth to keep myself from screaming, and I ran like
a bleedin' hare.'

Some poor devil really had got the horrors, but Harry's interest dwindled because it was unlikely that Doc Trenton was responsible. An unknown medical man had cut off the sufferer's supply of tranquillizers or pep pills and the withdrawal symptoms were at their height.

'I'm going nuts, Jim, and that's a fact. Naureen's in hospital, but after what happened I haven't been able to bring myself to go and see her. Naurie and I have been close since we was kids and now I hate her. I hope she's suffering like I am.' Harry heard the speaker choke back a sob. 'All the same it's hell being alone in the flat. Hell on earth, and I'll do myself in if those bastards come near me again. I just can't take no more, though I know I deserve to suffer.'

'Don't be daft, Fergus.' Another man spoke and Harry stiffened. 'The trouble's all in your mind, because you're feeling guilty about that job the three of you did. Why not tell me about it? They say confession's good for the soul.'

'You know that's impossible, Jim. You may be a pal, but this was something special and the three of us swore we'd never breathe a word about it.' The man paused again and Harry inclined his ear towards the knot-hole. The names told him who the first speaker was, and he recognized the voice of Fergus Carlin. The last time he'd heard that voice Carlin had been thanking a jury for acquitting him and his partner, Martin Starr, for a bank-robbery they had almost certainly committed.

'Not like any job we'd done before, I'll tell you that much. Room like a tiny chapel . . . crosses and symbols . . . something that might have been a holy water stoop . . . smell . . . smell of rubble and dust . . . the child on the cot . . . the loot there as we'd been promised . . . Naurie pulling out her knife and getting to work.' Carlin was rambling as much to himself as his companion, Harry could only make out the odd words, but those words didn't tally with what he knew about the man and his associates.

The Carlins and Martin Starr were a trio of professional crooks who were unlikely to be troubled by remorse. Also, Fergus Carlin's speciality was cat-burglary and he kept his body in good shape. He did not smoke, he drank sparingly, and certainly did not use drugs. So just what had caused his horrors?

'Crosses and a room like a chapel, Jim. Could we be guilty of sacrilege, maybe? Is God sending those things to punish me?' He spoke slightly louder and Harry pulled out his shorthand pad. 'Yes, that could be it. I was born a Catholic though I haven't been to church for years, and I believe that people are punished for really evil actions.'

There was a hint of hope in his tone. 'If that's what's happening to me, there's still a chance. You just said that confession's good for the soul and a priest might . . . might give me absolution. At least he'd listen and keep quiet afterwards, Jim.'

'He'd listen all right, but I don't know about absolution.' The other man was clearly sceptical. 'No harm in trying, though, and Father Mike O'Gorman down at Holy Innocents will be hearing confessions from twelve to three today. But these things aren't real Fergus. You're sick in your mind, and what you want is a doctor.'

'To hell with that. I've had enough of bloody doctors and only a priest can help me. You can't begin to understand what it's like waiting for those creatures to start on me and absolution's the one thing that can stop 'em. Yes, that's the way to lift the curse.' Carlin's hopes were rising and he spoke almost normally. 'Is this Father O'Gorman a decent sort of feller, Jim?'

'Sure, but he's not God, Fergus, and remember how the confession works. A priest can't split on you, but you won't get absolution just by saying a few Hail Marys; not if you've done something really nasty. You'll have to prove that you're truly penitent, and that might mean giving yourself up to the law.'

'Nasty . . . Yes, what we did was nasty right enough . . . nasty just about sums it up. What happened to that poor brat was really nasty.' The adjective had stuck in Carlin's mind. 'Very nasty indeed.

'I'm going to talk to O'Gorman, Jim. I'm going to tell him everything and if he won't help it'll be a razor or a high window for me. You say he starts hearing confessions at noon, so we've just got time for another couple of drinks.' There was a clink of coins on a table. 'You go to the bar and get 'em, there's a good

chap. My hands are shaking so badly that I'd spill half the stuff.'
Harry heard the second man ease back his chair and stand up,
and he followed suit. But he didn't go to the counter, though
he could have done with a stiff whisky to numb his conscience.
The telephone and the directories near the door were his goals.
He felt very guilty as he approached them, but he couldn't help
himself. He might be on to a story which would reinstate him
with John Forest, and curiosity outweighed morality, because
the key word was 'nasty'.

What crime had the Carlin-Starr gang committed that could
be described in such a way? They were professional crooks
and enemies of society who used violence when the need
arose. Martin Starr had once coshed a night watchman, Fergus
Carlin had threatened a bank clerk with a cut-throat razor,
and his sister had thrown pepper into a policeman's eyes. But
their acts had been motivated by gain, not malice or cruelty,
and they weren't perverted sadists. The implication was that
Naureen had attacked a child and that did not tally with their
past records. It was also out of character that a hard-bitten,
temperate burglar who kept himself in good condition should
suffer from imaginary horrors.

'Nasty,' Harry whispered while behind his contact lenses his
eyes ran over the L to R directory for the number of the Rev.
Michael O'Gorman. 'Very nasty indeed.'


The church was empty and with any luck Fergus Carlin should
be his first visitor. Harry had found a prayer book and a cassock
in the vestry, and he moved to the door of the confessional
box. Carlin had better be the first, he thought grimly. The man
had not practised his religion for twenty years, he would have
forgotten the form of service, but one of O'Gorman's regular
flock would be quite a different proposition. He settled himself in the booth and studied the Sacrament of Penance in the
dim light coming from a slit leading to an adjoining compartment. From where he sat he would be able to see the head and
shoulders of the penitent, but remain in shadow himself.

So far he had been lucky. His story on the telephone that he was a new arrival in the parish whose wife was on her deathbed had been accepted, though the priest had pleaded that he was without a curate and advised him to get in touch with another church. But when Harry had told him that he had done so and failed to obtain help, O'Gorman had agreed and was now on his way to a non-existent address. Harry had arrived in time to see him fix a sheet of paper to the church notice board stating that he would be unavailable for an hour and then pedal off on a bicycle with his gown flapping round his knees. Harry had waited till he was out of sight and then removed the message and entered the church.

Could such an action ever be justified? Harry was not a Christian and outside the building his conscience hadn't troubled him too badly. But now, in the dimly-lit box smelling of incense and furniture polish, and with his eyes facing the tiny window through which so many admissions of guilt and pleas for forgiveness had been made, his self-disgust rose and he dreaded the coming ordeal.

An ordeal that was on hand. The clock had struck the hour and as its chimes ended, he heard two pairs of footsteps moving down the aisle towards him. As they approached, Harry realized that the leading feet belonged to a woman and he prepared to throw in the sponge and beat his retreat. Trying to trick Fergus Carlin was one thing, because he was a felon who had been involved in an unpleasant crime. But he couldn't deceive an innocent third party. He had started to get up and move to the door when Carlin spoke.

'Excuse me, madam. Would you let me go first, please? I am in very deep distress.' There was silence for a moment, a mutter of thanks, and the click of the woman's shoes drawing aside. The curtain screening and the outer compartment parted and Fergus Carlin was standing before him.

'Bless me, Father, for I have sinned.' The floorboards creaked as he lowered himself on to his knees and Harry read a line from the prayer book and waited for him to continue. 'I confess to Almighty God . . . to the Virgin Mary . . . that I have sinned exceedingly in thought, word and deed.' The man was obviously racking his memory for the correct phrases. 'Especially I have sinned since my last confession which was long – very long ago.'

'What sins trouble you most grievously, my son?' Through the slit Harry caught a reek of Irish whisky on his breath and the smell of his body. The sour, bitter odour of sweat and adrenalin released by terror.

'A very terrible sin, Father, and I am paying for it now. I think I have been cursed for what happened and the things – those unspeakable things – have been sent to punish me.' He spoke in gasps and though Harry could not see his eyes he was certain they were weeping. 'Lift the curse, Father. Lift it quickly, because it's dark in here and they always come in the dark. Please give me absolution and say that I'm forgiven.'

'How can I absolve you till I know what you have done, my son?' Harry adopted a tone of kindly authority. 'What was the exact nature of your sin?'

'Robbery, Father, though that was the least of it. We were told we could have the jewels and all the other valuables, but in return we had to carry out our instructions and we did just that, Father. Naurie took out a knife and . . .' The words broke off in a fit of sobbing and Harry felt the compartment between them shake. 'Yes, Naurie used a knife and I let her. That's what must have brought on the curse. That's why God has sent those monsters – those snake-like brutes – to haunt me.'

'Snakes – never did like snakes. Give me the creeps – same as Marty hates rats.' He was speaking more to himself than to Harry. 'How Marty cursed during that Stepney warehouse job when a rat ran over his foot. Dead white he went and Naurie and I laughed at him.'

'You imagine that you are being tormented by snakes, my son.' He had fallen silent again and Harry prompted him. 'Tell me exactly what you did to deserve such torment.'

'Snakes, Father, but not real snakes.' Carlin ignored the question and rambled on. 'Their skin isn't dry and cold, but damp and soft and putrid. They're like entrails and they crawl over my body leaving their foul slime behind them.

'And they're coming now, Father. I can hear them and smell them and soon I'll feel them around me again.' Carlin's voice was shrill and frenzied. 'They are here in the church, before long they'll be wriggling under the curtain and I can't face the bastards any more. For the love of God absolve me, Father O'Gorman.'

'You will receive absolution when I have heard the full story. Who was the child and what did you and Naureen do to her, Carlin?' Harry stopped abruptly, but he knew he had revealed himself. The man must have heard the name and realized he'd been duped.

'Go on, my son.' Apart from a whimper there was silence beyond the slit. By some million-to-one chance his mistake had gone undetected and Harry continued. 'Tell me everything and you will be quite safe.'

'No, it's too late. Far too late, and there's no time left. No time at all.' Carlin spoke with the complete assurance of the insane. 'Goodbye O'Gorman you merciless swine, and may you share my agony one day.'

'Stop it, Carlin.' The words had been followed by a louder thud and it was Harry's turn to be afraid, because he understood what the abuse meant. 'You are forgiven, and the curse is lifted.' He shouted aloud and craned forward, but nobody heard him. The thick curtain screened the booth from the body of the church and the mysterious They had triumphed.

Fergus Carlin was slumped against the wall and he had two mouths. One was in the normal position while its neighbour lay below the chin and something resembling a toothbrush handle protruded from the scarlet lips. Carlin was dead and the razor that had severed his throat was still lodged in the wound.

# Chapter 3

'Hold her really tight. She must be kept quite still till I've found a vein.' Dr Miriam Stanford bent over the bed and its occupant struggled in desperation as she saw the glint of the hypodermic syringe.

'No, please, no. Don't take me there – not there. Not to One Hundred and One.' Froth dribbled from her lips and her eyes were glazed with terror. Though illness had weakened her, she was a big, powerful woman and it took the joint efforts of a nurse and two porters to hold her down.

'Stop worrying, my dear. You're just going to have a nice, deep sleep.' Miriam smiled reassuringly but she knew that verbal comfort was useless. The terrified eyes reminded her of a wounded rabbit waiting for the hunter to break its neck. 'You'll feel much better when you wake up.'

'And when I wake up, I'll be there won't I? I'll have to look at the . . . the thing . . . you've . . .' The morphine had reached her brain, the words stopped, the lids flickered over the pupils and the limbs relaxed.

'That should put her out for about three hours.' Miriam straightened and laid aside the syringe. 'Ample time for them to take further X-rays and make the other tests I want. If she becomes violent again when this injection wears off, the duty officer had better give her another shot.'

'I'll tell him, Dr Stanford.' The nurse had swabbed the puncture in the patient's arm and she stood aside to let the porters lift her inert body on to a trolley. A few seconds ago the woman's features had been hideously contorted, but in repose they had a certain dignity, though her face was not beautiful or even handsome. A heavy, big-boned face which did not suggest its owner was over-imaginative. 'What do you think the fresh tests will tell you, Doctor?'

'God knows, Alice. I'd have bet my last penny that the earlier X-rays would have shown she had a tumour or a cerebral haemorrhage, but there was no sign of any physiological damage. If the new results are also negative, it'll be a question of narco-analysis when her fever subsides.' The porters had wheeled out the trolley and Miriam picked up a clip-board. 'I was quite certain that the cause of her disturbance must be physical, because paranoid schizophrenia almost always reveals its presence at an early age. Our patient is thirty-six, and according to her own G.P. she is not at all neurotic and has never suffered from any mental trouble.' Miriam replaced the board on a hook at the foot of the bed and sighed. She had practised psychiatry for over three years and knew that she was good at her job. But if the patient's doctor was correct, and if the second tests revealed no physical disturbance, she hadn't a clue what was wrong with the woman.

'Excuse me, Doctor.' A sister had appeared in the doorway of the little private ward. 'Your patient's brother has called to inquire about her and he's waiting at Reception.'

'Then I'd better see him straight away. Though her doctor believes she was well-balanced, neurotics are excellent actors, and she might have deceived him. But a close relative couldn't have been deceived for long and the brother might tell a different story.

'Thank you, Sister Jackson.' Miriam hurried away down the corridor considering the case. The patient was obviously suffering from acute persecution mania, and so far they had found nothing suggestive of brain damage. If that was true her condition was mental and this attack could hardly have been the first. The neurotic fantasies would have been building up over a long period and had come to a head when she woke up in strange surroundings. The brother must have noticed traces of her delusions and he might just know what had started them.

'Mr Carlin?' She had reached the reception hall and walked over to a man standing by the desk. He nodded on hearing the name and she held out her hand. I am Dr Stanford – Miriam Stanford – and I have just been examining your sister.'

'It's very kind of you to see me so promptly, Doctor.' Harry adopted an Irish accent. Though Fergus Carlin was not known at the hospital, he could see that Miriam would be a difficult person to fool. She was still in her twenties, but her manner was brisk and self-possessed and her eyes and slightly Jewish features were disconcertingly intelligent. All the same, she was going to be fooled, because 'In for a penny – in for a pound' had to be his motto from now on. A man had cut his throat because he was too frightened to go on living, and Harry was determined to follow the story through and discover the cause of Carlin's terrors. 'How is Naureen, Dr Stanford?'

'Rather poorly, and I'm glad of a chance to talk to you.' For some reason her visitor's face seemed very familiar, but Miriam couldn't recall where she had seen him before. 'Shall we find somewhere to sit down?' A waiting-room adjoined the hall and she led the way to two quiet corner seats.

'As you know, your sister was admitted here yesterday after-noon, Mr Carlin, after collapsing in the street. Her life was in some danger and she showed the characteristic symptoms of food-poisoning: cramp, fever and sickness.

'But no poison was found in her stomach, and it then seemed probable that some virus infection had caused her col-lapse. Another wrong diagnosis, I'm afraid.' Miriam paused for a moment. The man looked as hard as nails, but what she was going to say might distress him. 'Your sister's trouble ap-pears to come from the mind, Mr Carlin, and I am a psycholo-gist.'

'I don't understand you.' Though Harry lied convincingly, he was beginning to understand a great deal, and the scene in the confessional box raced through his brain. The police would be examining Carlin's body now. After leaving the church he had telephoned them without giving his name, and then rung a number of hospitals till he found where Naureen had been admitted. Now the pieces of the puzzle were clicking together in a rush. The brother had died during a brainstorm, and the sister was being treated by a psychiatrist. 'I knew Naureen was in a bad way, because they told me she couldn't have any visitors, but you're saying that she's mad – insane. Just what's wrong with her, Dr Stanford?'

'We don't know, but you may be able to help us find out, Mr Carlin.' Again Miriam had the sensation that they had met before. 'Your sister is still feverish, but her other physical symptoms soon disappeared after she was brought here and it seems likely that they were psychosomatic. Bodily malfunctions brought about by extreme mental stress. The stress persists, however, and we have not been able to find any sign of brain damage, though further tests are being made now. In view of the situation, I'd like to ask you a few questions and I hope you will answer them frankly.' She took a pencil and a notebook from her jacket. 'Does your sister drink heavily and is she addicted to drugs?'

'Not to the best of my knowledge.' Harry's excitement rose while she noted his answer and a solution to the mystery occurred to him. He had first thought that Carlin was suffering from withdrawal symptoms, and discarded the idea because of the man's character and record. But it was possible that both the Carlins had been drugged without their knowledge. Hepped-up to do a job they would never have undertaken in normal circumstances.

'In her youth did your sister suffer from night terrors or delusions of persecution?' He shook his head and Miriam made another note. 'Has she recently had any traumatic experience? A severe shock that could have disturbed her mind?'

'That's possible, Doctor, though Naureen is pretty cagey and I don't know any details.' The question brought Harry back to the other possible solution. Night terrors – Fergus Carlin had had those. The snake-like horrors which made their appearance in darkness and dim light, and had finally killed him. Surely more than drugs were involved. Something that occurred during the robbery – the Carlins' last job – had destroyed their reason. 'But I think it's my turn to question you, Dr Stanford,' he said. 'Could a shock have produced the symptoms you mentioned? Cramp, vomiting and so forth?'

'Easily, because the body is very much influenced by

the mind, but your sister's case is more severe than any I've known.' Miriam lowered her pencil. She intended to probe into the family background and mental history but that could wait. The man was the patient's next of kin and it was his right to be put in the picture. 'You will find what I'm going to tell you depressing, Mr Carlin, so please smoke if you wish.

'Not just now, thank you.' He had offered her a cigarette, but she shook her head and waited till he had lit one himself. 'When it was clear that your sister had not been poisoned, she was given antibiotics and a mild sedative and put to bed. She slept well at first, but in the early hours of the morning the other patients complained that she was muttering loudly, and the night nurse woke her up.

'Since then Naureen has completely retreated from reality. She has no idea where she is and thinks the hospital is a place of punishment – a prison or a concentration camp. In the X-ray department she seemed to believe she was about to be tortured and kept whimpering and repeating a string of disjointed words. Cell and tomb – stone and tar, were some of them. Also a number – one hundred and one.

'Do the words convey something to you?' Harry was staring hard at her and Miriam noticed his eyes. Naureen Carlin's doctor had said that her brother was a building-contractor. It was slightly eccentric of him to wear contact lenses.

'Not the words, but the number might be significant.' Harry dragged at his cigarette to control his excitement. 'What else did Naureen say?'

'Very little, and none of it was rational.' Miriam looked at her watch. 'The real crisis came an hour ago. After leaving X-ray, your sister was put in a private ward and she overpowered the nurse in attendance and tried to break out of the hospital. They had quite a struggle getting her back to bed and she was still raving before I gave her a morphine injection. Repeating that number and rambling on about a cell where something unspeakable is waiting for her.'

'So it is, Doctor, though the place is not a cell, but a room – an interrogation room.' The penny had dropped in Harry's

mind and he forgot the assumed Irish brogue. 'The occupants
of Room One Hundred and One are too frightful to be named.'

'Thank you. I remember the quotation now.' The change of
accent had given him away and Miriam's own voice was sharp
and angry. She realized that she had never met the self-styled
Fergus, but she knew who he was now. His name and photograph had once appeared on a newspaper beside the account
of a sensational murder case.

'Room One Hundred and One contains the worst thing in
the world, Mr Clay.'

'A chapel that smelled of rubble – crosses and other symbols –
a holy water stoop.' Miriam's anger had given way to curiosity.
'Three burglars; the Carlins and a man named Starr recently
committed a crime and two of them are now terrified out of
their wits. Have you any idea what the crime was, Mr Clay?'

'Not yet, but I intend to find out. That's why I came here
impersonating Naureen's brother.' Harry had told her about
Fergus Carlin's horrors, but he had not mentioned his impos-
ture of a priest or the man's suicide. His story was that he had
heard everything through the bar partition, followed Carlin
when he left the pub and lost him in the street. 'Robbery took
place, a child was involved, and Carlin seemed to think sacrilege had been committed. He and his sister were once Catho-
lics. If they had robbed a church and stolen religious relics or
ornaments could that account for their condition, Doctor?'

'Guilts strong enough to sentence them both to Room
One Hundred and One, the sinister creation of a writer called
George Orwell.' They had moved to the hospital canteen and
Miriam sipped at a cup of black coffee. 'Orwell's premise was
that every human being is haunted by one cardinal fear, and
that is what the room contains. A horror that varies from individual to individual.' Miriam remembered the agony in her
patient's eyes before the morphine closed them. 'We all have
our own personal fears. Some of us dread painful forms of
death – impalement, drowning, being buried alive. Others are
frightened by living creatures – spiders, reptiles, rats. But each

of us has one terror that is unendurable. The worst thing in the world.'

'Fergus Carlin feared snakes. Snakes like entrails.' Harry quoted. ' "Damp and soft and putrid. They crawl over my body leaving their foul slime behind them." I wonder what was Naureen's bugbear.'

'She didn't even dare to name it, Mr Clay.' Miriam looked at the canteen clock. The test results should be available by now and she would soon know if her patient's illness had a physical cause. 'The film of *Nineteen Eighty-Four* was reshown on television not long ago and I suppose Naureen must have seen it or read the book. In either event, the Room One Hundred and One situation has stuck in her mind and it is the only way she can describe her terrors.'

'Is there no method to get her to talk? Hypnosis, perhaps?'

'Narco-analysis might, but that's a tricky business when the subject is as distressed as Naureen Carlin.' Miriam's irritation towards Harry returned, and not because he had deceived her. His suggestion that two hardened criminals had shared a joint experience which was strong enough to derange them offended all her personal beliefs and professional training. 'The woman will only have narco-analysis as a last resort, Mr Clay, because I don't share your suspicions. You're implying that the Carlins are not merely tortured with remorse. You want a lurid story, and you've started to believe that divine retribution is involved. Spiritual punishment for what was done, and that's mumbo-jumbo. The two-headed devil howling away on the ruined church and something nasty in the woodshed.

'I will go along with one possibility you put forward, though. The Carlins may be suffering the after-effects of some drug that was administered without their knowledge. If that's true, they will recover of their own accord as soon as those effects have worn off.

'Thank you.' A messenger had hurried across to their table and handed her a cardboard folder. 'With any luck this should tell us what's wrong with the woman.' Miriam opened the folder and studied its contents. Photographs and chemical data and the notes of technicians. 'No, there is no tumour or cerebral haemorrhage, and her brain appears to be physically normal. No trace of drugs in the blood stream either, apart from what she has received here. And that just doesn't make sense, unless . . .' Miriam frowned and then reread an entry aloud. ' "An abnormal percentage of adrenalin in the vascular system suggests that the adrenal glands have been over-activated by intense mental stress." '

'Fair enough. She was under stress, but I wonder – just wonder if the cart hasn't been put before the horse and the stress was not a cause but a symptom.' Miriam lowered the papers and sat silent for a moment before she continued.

'Her doctor stated that Naureen does not suffer from any chronic illness, but she may do, and so may her brother. An inherited condition similar to epilepsy, which only reveals itself on rare occasions and affects the adrenal glands. Should that be true, we can say goodbye to your bogeymen, Mr Clay.' Harry's expression had become wan and she grinned.

'I'm sure you know that adrenalin is a drug manufactured by our own bodies. A pep-up that creates tension and stimulates the imagination. If the Carlins' disease produces sudden and really excessive quantities of adrenalin in the system, that could account for their symptoms, Harry.'

'It might indeed, Miriam.' She had used his first name automatically and it was Harry's turn to smile. 'But I very much hope you're wrong, because I like bogeymen – bogeymen are my stock-in-trade, and your solution has no news value. But it has got a thumping great flaw. If this mysterious malady only comes into the open at rare intervals, it's too much of a coincidence that both brother and sister should be taken ill simultaneously.' Harry eased back his chair.

'You may be right, of course, and there's a simple way to validate your theory or prove that there is something nasty in the woodshed – a demon behind the door numbered One Hundred and One.

'The Carlins are blood relations. They may share an inherited illness, but they definitely share something else. They have a partner.' Harry's smile widened as he stood up. 'I want to know what's the worst thing in the world for Marty Starr.'

# Chapter 4

At first Harry imagined that a car had backfired and the crowd was assembled for some rally or demonstration. But as he drew nearer he realized that he was wrong. The people blocking the road had no political axe to grind, and no intention of pushing past the police cordon. The police were there to protect them and he had not heard any backfiring. Apart from three stationary vehicles, the street beyond the cordon was clear of traffic and the sound had been a shot. As he edged his way through the bystanders, there was a second report followed by a man's voice shouting hoarsely and indistinctly from somewhere around the corner.

'Why don't they put in the dogs?' 'Let the bastard have a sniff of tear gas.' The crowd was both excited and apprehensive like spectators watching a bull-fight or a motor-race behind frail barriers. 'What if he tries to shoot his way out down here?'

'He won't kill her, will he officer?' 'He don't really mean what he says.' Harry was almost up to the police and he saw a woman sobbing and clutching a sergeant's arm. 'He always seemed so fond of our Mary, that's why I let her do his shopping. Like an uncle to Mary he was, and he knows she has to have them pills.'

'Inspector – Inspector Munro.' A familiar figure stood studying a street-map and Harry called out to him. He had once given Munro a flattering write-up in the *Globe* and the inspector might believe that one good turn deserved another. 'Please put me in the picture, Mr Munro.'

'Ah, the first vulture has flown in from Fleet Street.' The policeman regarded him coldly and then nodded to the sergeant. 'You can let him through, Latham.

'The picture, as you flippantly call it, Mr Clay, is an increas-

ingly common one these days.' Munro's tone was irritable. 'A
lunatic has barricaded himself in his flat with a rifle and an
automatic pistol for company. The pistol has already killed a
dog and one of my chaps has been carted off to hospital with
a rifle bullet in his thigh.

'And apart from his armoury, the bastard has a hostage –
a little girl of ten. Daughter of that poor soul behind you.'
Under a grim exterior the inspector was a kind-hearted man
and his expression softened at the distraught woman. 'The
child used to go shopping for the joker now and again, and on
her way home from school she called to see if he wanted anything. Pity she picked the very moment he went crazy.' Munro
looked at the map while he talked.

'Starr – that's the fellow's name, was supposed to be fond
of the lass, but now he's got her standing up in front of the
window and threatens to blow her brains out if we rush him.'

'It is Starr, then?' While he was on the *Globe* Harry had made
several underworld contacts, and a telephone call had supplied
him with his quarry's address. Munro's statement proved that
Miriam Stanford was wrong, he thought. Hereditary illness
was not involved because the Carlins' partner shared their
horrors. 'The Martin Starr who was acquitted of the Croydon
bank job, Inspector?'

'Don't be daft, Mr Clay.' Munro snorted contemptuously,
folded the map and started to walk towards a group of police-
men stationed at the next corner. 'It's not that Starr – not on
your nellie. Marty's a villain and a ruddy nuisance who ought
to be under lock and key, but he's no nut-case, and it's another
star we've got to pull out of some crazy heaven. Just listen to
him.'

'Keep 'em away, I tell you . . . can't stand the sight of those
. . . those filthy, diseased vermin.' The man was shouting again,
but a wall deflected his words and Harry could not make out
all he said. 'I'll kill her . . . kill her . . . kill little Mary.'

'You'll do no such thing, Mr Starr. You're very fond of Mary
Seaton and you couldn't harm her even if you wanted to.' Another voice boomed out from the loudspeaker of a police van.

'And nobody wants to harm you either, so come to your senses. Put down those guns and lower the child out of the window.'

'Damn you.' The sound of a shot silenced the loudspeaker and the insane voice screamed in fury. 'Liars . . . all of you . . . bloody sadistic liars. I know you – I know what you want to do to me, but I'll shoot her first. Mary's a nice kid, but I can't . . . can't stand those monsters.'

'He may kill her, too. The chap's as mad as a hatter, and do you know what drove him crazy?' Munro pointed at a rather tragic tableau on the opposite pavement. An elderly man crouched beside the dead body of a grey-muzzled sheepdog.

'Exactly twenty-seven pounds and ten new pence sent Starr off his rocker.' The inspector noted the disbelief in Harry's expression. 'It's true enough, Mr Clay. That old fellow is Vickers, a rent collector and he always takes the dog with him on his rounds, because this is a tough neighbourhood and he has to carry a lot of cash.

'Well, he called for the tenants' monthly instalments this afternoon, and when Starr opened the door he didn't seem to recognize him. Appeared completely bewildered after Vickers asked him for the money and then he looked at the dog, gave a sort of whimper and produced his pistol. Shot the poor brute through the head and told Vickers to take it out of his sight, or he'd get the same treatment.

'And all for twenty-seven pounds and ten pence.' The amount seemed to fascinate Munro. 'That rules out the Martin Starr you had in mind, Mr Clay. Our Marty wouldn't give a damn about that kind of money.'

'Whoever he is, his mania takes a pretty strange form.' Harry was looking at the rent collector who remained bent over the dead animal with a hand stroking its bloodstained head. A long, narrow head with overshot jaws and teeth that still appeared menacing in death. 'The man's homicidal, so why did he shoot the dog – not its master?'

'That's obvious, I'd have thought.' Harry felt certain that the point was vital, but the inspector shrugged it aside. 'A big collie's more of a threat than an old man in his seventies and

Starr probably imagined Vickers would set the dog on him if he didn't pay up.' They had reached the group of police-men and Munro halted. 'But you're right about the homicidal tendencies, and I told you that he did shoot a man. Constable Triggs, the bobby on the beat, tried to reason with him before anybody knew he'd got the child in the flat, and Starr fired a warning shot and then put a bullet into his leg.'

'I've still got a hunch that it's Marty Starr, the bank-robber.' Harry considered telling Munro that his hunch was a certainty, but decided against it. The inspector would be interested to know why he was so sure, and at a later date his questioning might turn to the death of Fergus Carlin. 'May I borrow your glasses and have a look at the man? I covered Starr's trial and I'd recognize him again.'

'By all means, though you'll see nothing recognizable.' Munro grinned wryly and removed a pair of binoculars from his shoulders. 'And don't stay in sight for long unless you fancy a trip to the morgue.'

'Thanks for the loan and the warning.' Harry took the glasses from him and moved past the seven men who formed Munro's advance guard. Two were holding Alsatian dogs on short leads, three carried rifles, one had a walkie-talkie radio, and one was stationed beside a tear-gas mortar.

'I understand why you smiled, Inspector.' Harry had craned round the corner. The block of flats was at the end of a cul-de-sac and about two hundred yards distant. The evening sun shone on its windows and a small, fair-haired girl stood on one of the windowsills. The binoculars showed that her mouth was open as though she was screaming, but Harry knew that she couldn't scream. In her panic she was gasping for breath and her face made him think of a theatrical mask portraying terror. There was a rubber-gloved hand on her shoulder and behind the hand he saw another mask which portrayed nothing at all. A blurred, metallic visor like something out of a science-fiction film.

'What is he wearing on his face, Inspector?' Harry had seen enough and he drew back. 'A fencing-guard?'

'Nothing so sophisticated.' Munro frowned at his watch. 'The thing appears to be an ordinary kitchen strainer fixed in position by tape. The fellow may be mad, but he can't be fool enough to think wire mesh will stop bullets.'

'I don't believe he's worried about bullets.' Harry handed him the binoculars. 'The wire is intended to stop something less lethal, but far more repulsive.'

'The chaps are in position, Benson?' Munro had ignored Harry's comment and he lowered his watch and spoke to the man with the radio set. 'You've told 'em that they'll have to go in soon?'

'They're ready and waiting, sir.' The constable was very young and his expression showed strain and uncertainty. 'But what happens if they do try to tackle him? What about the kid?'

'That's not your concern, lad. Just follow orders.' Munro looked at his watch again and turned to Harry. 'I'm no psychologist, Mr Clay. I don't know why Starr's strapped a strainer round his head, but this I do know.' He nodded at the rifles and the mortar. 'In exactly seven minutes we must start shooting to create a diversion while another squad tries to break in through the back door of the flat and rush him.'

'Which will probably cost a child's life, Inspector.' Harry's eyes widened with astonishment. 'The man's out of his mind. He's beside himself with fear and he'll kill that girl as soon as he hears your men at the door. Why not wait till he gets hungry or thirsty and then . . .'

'Don't tell me my duty.' Munro was still staring at the hurrying minute-hand of his watch. 'What you suggest would be the normal course of action, Mr Clay, and preparations have already been made. The pipe joining Starr's water cistern to the mains has been broached, and if he runs off one gallon to clear the tank and then takes a drink he'll be out cold. There's enough tranquilliser – Destrophine K – in the water to put an elephant to sleep.

'But he may not have a thirst and we can't wait for him to develop one. That child, Mary Seaton suffers from . . .'

'Mr Starr, you must see reason.' The loudspeaker interrupted Munro and made his explanation unnecessary. 'Mary
suffers from *status asthmaticus* and she must take steroid pills
every six hours. Without those pills she could suffocate to
death and it is over seven hours since her last dosage. You
know that, Starr. You know that Mary needs those pills . . .
that she will die without them, so for the love of God let her
go.' The man at the microphone would have done well on the
stage and his message was vibrant with emotion. 'If you refuse
to release Mary at least allow us to bring the pills across to
her.'

'No, damn you.' The voice echoed from the buildings. 'I
know what you want to bring me. Not pills – not medicine.
They're with you – They're waiting – It's them you hope to
bring, so keep back – Don't let them come near me.'

He had killed the dog, not its master. The shouts had
stopped and Harry looked at the police Alsatians. Like the dead
collie one of them had a long, overshot muzzle resembling a
rodent's and while he watched it he seemed to hear Fergus
Carlin moaning in the confessional. 'Snakes – like entrails.'
Those were the horrors that had driven Carlin to suicide and
Harry had no doubts about the cause of Starr's breakdown,
because Carlin had said something else. 'How Marty cursed
during that Stepney warehouse job.' Harry knew why the
collie had been shot now. He knew the reason for those rubber
gloves. He knew what lurked in Room One Hundred and One
for Marty Starr.

'Inspector Munro,' he said. 'I covered the Croydon case, I
sat through the trial and I interviewed the man after his ac-
quittal. I am quite certain that that was Marty Starr's voice we
heard just now, so please listen carefully. I also know what his
phobia is and there may be a way to free that child without
using violence.'

'Then let's hear it quickly, because time's almost up.' Munro
listened impatiently and when Harry finished he was clearly
sceptical about the madman's identity and the proposed plan
of action. 'That's an off-beat theory if ever I heard one, Mr

Clay. You honestly believe that an aversion – a dislike – can snowball into actual terror?

'Yes, I suppose it's a possibility, though a darned unlikely one.' He fell silent for a moment and Harry saw that his scepticism was on the wane. 'I don't like cats myself. The bastards give me the creeps when they rub against my legs.

'The idea's worth a try, maybe – worth a risk, I should say. If you're right and we scare him too badly, that girl could still end up with her brains spattering the windowsill. But that could happen if we rush him and she'll die in any case unless she gets the medicine soon.' Munro had made up his mind and he turned to the radio-operator.

'There's a change of plan, Benson, so contact the squad behind the building and give 'em these orders. They're to keep away from the door and line up against the wall of the flat. They will wait there in complete silence till they hear my voice on the loudspeaker. When that happens they will start scraping the brickwork and make as much noise as they can.

'Scrape the wall with what?' The man had asked a question and he repeated it scornfully. 'They've been issued with guns and given jemmies to force the door. They also have handcuffs and truncheons. Tell them to use anything they like, but make a real racket.

'And you two can keep on your toes when the transmission starts.' He addressed the dog-handlers. 'If he leaves the child, go in after him.

'Right, Mr Clay. This is your scheme, so cross your fingers and wish us luck.'

'My fingers have never been more tightly crossed, Inspector.' Munro had climbed into the van and Harry moved towards the street corner. In his mind's eye he could see the slumped figure of Fergus Carlin on the church floor. Would Carlin still be alive if a real priest had been there to comfort him, he wondered, and then considered a more pressing question. Would Mary Seaton die if his plan failed or worked too well?

'You're not mad, Starr – you're just a bloody fool.' The inspector's voice rasped from the loudspeaker, and Harry craned round the wall. 'You don't really imagine that those creatures need our help to get at you, Starr. They can come on their own and they're on their way now. Have you forgotten that they can gnaw through timber and concrete and brickwork? Don't you know that they hate open spaces and love the dark? The darkness of the sewers, Starr, and it's up from the sewers that they're coming.' Munro's tone was as harsh as the horrors he was conjuring up. 'So stop looking out of the window, Starr, because you'll see nothing. Turn round and listen, Starr. Listen to their claws and their teeth. Listen to the music of the rats.'

The inspector stopped and Harry dashed forward because the scheme had taken effect. Starr was screaming and cursing and shots were being fired. Two shots in quick succession, followed by a third and a fourth, but Harry ignored them. There was nobody at the window now, Mary Seaton had jumped from the sill and the bullets were not intended for her or for him. Marty Starr had no ammunition to waste on human targets. He was defending himself from the worst things in the world.

With his breath coming in gasps and his heart racing, Harry pounded on, and though he was out of training he'd never run faster in his life. The policemen were far behind him, the building was looming over him and the girl was staggering towards him with her arms outstretched for help. She looked completely exhausted, but had not been wounded and Harry swerved to avoid her and made for the window. A fifth report rang out when he reached it and a sixth blasted his eardrums as he vaulted over the sill and stood panting in the room of the flat.

Martin Starr was a professional criminal, but till recently he had been an orderly and rather artistic person. His furniture was in the best of taste, the pictures on the walls were good reproductions of old masters and a bowl of hyacinths bloomed on a well-polished table. Apart from the wall facing the window, which was pockmarked with bullet holes, everything was neat and tidy, and on a desk near the window lay a collection of glittering objects. Starr must have been inspecting the spoils of the robbery when his mania began and he had neglected to replace them. But beside the collection was a sheet of foolscap paper and one glance told Harry that it might contain the key to the story – the information for which he was risking his life.

'Back – back – keep back.' The automatic roared again and Harry edged towards the desk. Starr was standing before the far wall and he was quite oblivious to anything except the scratching, scraping sounds that came from behind it.

'Back, you devils. Keep away from me I tell you.' The man never saw Harry slip the paper into his pocket, but he turned his head very slowly when the scratching noise ended and he heard a voice address him.

'Relax, Starr. We're friends and we've come to help you.' The policeman stood before the window but he made no move to enter the flat, and spoke kindly. 'There's nothing to be frightened of, so be a good chap and drop your gun.'

'Help me! No one can help me, you fool, and I'm damned – damned forever.' Through the wire mesh mask Harry could see the agony in Starr's eyes and he could also smell the agony. Mingled with the cordite fumes and the stench of flowers was the reek of Starr's body. The same sour stench of terror which had clung to Fergus Carlin in the curtained box.

'Drop that pistol.' The policeman had repeated his order, but it was ignored and Harry braced himself. Starr had not noticed him yet and he might be able to reach his arm before he fired.

'Only one bullet left.' The man straightened his shoulders and raised the gun to his head. A figure that was both sinister and pathetic with his rubber gloves, and the strainer over his face, and trouser bottoms tucked into his socks, as Harry had guessed they would be. 'One bullet to give me peace.'

'Stop it, Marty.' Harry threw himself across the room as a gloved finger tightened on the trigger, but his intervention could not save Starr. Another order had been given. A long, brown, overshot muzzle appeared at the window and the Alsatian bounded over the sill.

Marty Starr was doomed to die, though no more shots were fired. He gave a final despairing cry, the gun dropped from his grasp, and his body crumpled to the floor. Fear killed Starr and his heart had stopped before either Harry or the dog reached him.

## Chapter 5

'Miss Carlin has been put on the danger list, Nurse? I'm extremely sorry to hear that.' Paul Trenton was making a telephone call and he didn't look sorry at all; he looked delighted.

'Complications have set in, you say? That is bad news. Tch-tch-tch—' His tongue clicked sympathetically, but his eyes were bright with malice. 'Who is in charge of the case, Nurse?

'Ah, Dr Miriam Stanford.' He nodded at the answer. 'I know Dr Stanford by reputation and I'm sure Miss Carlin is having the best possible treatment. Please give her my good wishes for a speedy recovery. My name is . . .' He hesitated for an instant and then smiled. 'Savage – Edward Savage.'

'Miriam Stanford, eh.' Trenton's companion laid aside an evening paper as he lowered the receiver. 'Naureen is in the hands of a psychiatrist, which suggests that things are turning out as we expected.'

'Quite so, and though Miriam Stanford is an able girl, I think she may find the case rather beyond her capabilities. If I had any real money, I'd wager every penny that poor, dear Naureen is on the way out. Any medico worth his salt knows that 70 per cent of all physical illness stems from up here.' Trenton tapped his forehead. 'If the spirit loses the will to fight, the body also surrenders.'

'The news means that we have one down, one groggy, and one to go.' The woman glanced at a vacuum flask on a table beside her chair. 'The guardian of the treasure is still active and that little container holds a power which has haunted the western world from Donegal to Japan since the beginning of human history.'

'Exactly, dear lady, and that power is ours now. We have the means to revenge every insult and humiliation – to wipe the slate clean.' Trenton picked up the paper. 'After receiving an anonymous phone call the police find the body of Fergus Carlin in a church confessional box. The priest in charge, Father Michael O'Gorman, stated that shortly before he was due to hear confessions a hoaxer summoned him to a non-existent deathbed. In spite of this hoax and despite the fact that Carlin died of throat injuries, foul play is not suspected.

'The wound was self-inflicted in fact.' Trenton put the paper on the table and took a pipe from his pocket. 'I'd like to know who made those calls, though. The police are not infallible and it might only be murder.'

'Which would be disappointing, Doctor.' The woman left her chair and wandered idly around the room. 'But there is no need to worry, because I am certain the man did kill himself. He was a born Catholic and he thought a priest might be able to help him. But no priest was available so he . . .' She drew a finger across her throat and looked at the flask again.

'Destiny has led us, my friend. We did not meet by accident at that seance, nor was it accidental that you mentioned your interest in the legend just after I had started to suspect the true nature of the treasure. We have been guided from the beginning, and, provided you are what I hope and believe you to be, the last laugh will belong to us.

'How I shall enjoy laughing.' She halted before a bookcase. Most of the volumes were standard medical works, but a few of them aroused her interest; *Vampirism in Western Europe – The Book of the Werewolf – A History of the Essex Witch Trials*. She pulled out the last title and quoted a passage. ' "I shall seek safety with the Lord of the Dawn from the evil he has made, and from the darkness when it gathers." Odd that an eighteenth-century English clergyman should advocate words from the Koran as a protection.'

'Odd and also pathetic, because there is no safety.' Trenton had got the pipe drawing well and his eyes twinkled. 'If you have courage and faith, that darkness will return.'

'I need neither quality, Doctor. The blood of my ancestors will shield me like a screen and all I need is faith in you.' She replaced the book and nodded towards a radio. 'But the Carlins did not enter the house alone, so let us see if there is more confirmation.'

'That concludes our concert and it is time for the news summary.' Trenton had switched on the set and they heard a final burst of music followed by an announcer's voice. 'There is still no trace of the Boeing 707 airliner which vanished during a flight between Lisbon and New York yesterday . . . The death toll caused by the Turkish flood disaster is still mounting – so far eight hundred and nine bodies have been recovered. Hope is fading for the three miners trapped in Whitton-over-Wear colliery.'

Troubles in the sky – troubles on the ground – troubles under the earth. The major tragedies poured out, but there were plenty of lesser misfortunes to follow. A royal duke had broken his collar-bone playing polo. A politician had been injured in a motor accident. A rock climber had died in North Wales.

Finally, the item they had hoped for. 'At Porton Mansions in South London this afternoon, a man named Martin Starr had a mental breakdown, and, after wounding a police constable, locked himself in his flat holding a neighbour's child as a hostage. Starr died of a heart attack when a police-dog entered the premises, and the child, a girl of ten, escaped without injury.'

'And that is that, dear lady.' Trenton switched off the radio and crossed to a sideboard with little dancing steps. 'I am a poor man with a poor cellar, but I can offer you whisky, gin or sherry to toast our enterprise.'

'No toasts yet.' Trenton's expression was gleeful, but the woman's had become cold. 'Every chain has a weak link and before we proceed further I want to know if you are a fool or a knave, Mr Trenton.' She stressed his lack of medical title. 'You were struck off the register for incompetence, which means foolishness, and I do not suffer fools gladly.'

'You are quite right not to do so.' Trenton was quite un-
abashed by what she had said and he grinned as he mixed himself a gin and angostura. 'Only one member of the medical
council considered that I was a knave, madam, and he didn't
mince his words. "Criminal psychopath – a man who has dedicated himself to evil," were some of the terms he used, and
though the president rebuked him they were justified.' Trenton knocked back his drink in a single, practised movement
and walked over to a desk. 'I am a knave, dear lady, and what I
did to my patients was quite deliberate. Here are the fruits of
my labours.' He handed her two photographs.

'The Countess of Seaford was a beautiful creature before
she damaged her face on the hunting-field and came to me for
treatment. Such a pity that the nurse failed to sterilize my in-
struments thoroughly and septicaemia set in. So sad that I was
out of London when the inflammation flared up and her own
doctor had to reopen the incisions I'd made. A great shame
that he wasn't a plastic surgeon. In the second picture you can
see how disfiguring the scar tissue is.

'More of my handiwork, madam.' He held out two other
prints. 'Mrs Carlton also had been a beauty, but she was growing old. A vain woman, who wasn't content to be merely handsome. She wanted me to turn her into a girl again and I filled
out her cheeks with jelly. Unfortunately the stuff was of the
wrong consistency and it ran.' His tongue clicked sympathetically as it had done over the telephone. 'The poor thing's face
became all lopsided.

'Why did I risk being sued and struck off the register?' He
considered her question. 'I suppose that anger was my main
motivation. The countess is a loudmouthed, outspoken bitch,
and after I examined her and fixed a date for the operation we
happened to be fellow guests at a dinner party. I heard her mention my name to a friend and say this.' Trenton's urbanity vanished. ' "I'm sure the man's an excellent surgeon, but it's not
the knife that worries me. His *breath* darling – how it stinks." '

'So it does, Doctor – it stinks vilely.' The woman stared at
the photographs. 'How did Mrs Carlton offend you?'

'She didn't – it was her husband.' Trenton walked back to
the sideboard. 'He came to the nursing-home with her and I
didn't recognize him at first. I couldn't place him until it was
almost time for the operation and then everything came back.
We'd been at school together and he used to bully me – bully
me unmercifully.' Trenton's hands shook as he slopped more
gin into his glass. 'Once the bastard sat on my face and broke
wind.'

'Very objectionable, but not the true motivation.' The
woman crossed over to him and smiled warmly. 'Like myself,
you are possessed, Dr Trenton. A woodworm destroys timber
because that is its way of life, and you destroy beauty because
destruction is your mission. We are two of a kind, so pour me
out some sherry and we will have our toast.

'Thank you.' She took the glass from him, but before drinking she picked up the newspaper again and turned to the
entertainment advertisements. 'In two days' time Dame Susan
Vallance makes her comeback, so here's to her. Here's to *Our
Lady of Pain*.' She raised the glass ceremoniously.

'To Susan Vallance – damn her eyes.'


'Are you a fool or a knave, Harry?' John Forest echoed the
woman's question on a telephone line. 'You were not merely
the only reporter present, but the first person to enter Starr's
flat. Your role might almost be described as heroic, so why
the unprintable, unmentionable hell didn't you get your copy
through to the news desk straight away?'

'Because I wanted to talk to you personally, John, and until
now the switchboard kept telling me you were engaged.' Harry
felt that he had the whip hand and he was enjoying the experience. 'But I did send in my copy, as it happens. The *South-
West London Guardian and Advertiser* knows all about Alderman
Breakspear's memorial plaque.'

'Don't try to be funny, Harry.' The receiver rasped fero-
ciously. 'I know your game all right. You're hoping to provoke
me aren't you? You hope I'll fire you and you've promised an
eye-witness account of the Starr business to one of our rivals

– the *Examiner* or the *Blast*. But it won't work lad, because I'm not riled that easily and we'll sue. We'll have your press card and your union membership cancelled and as far as journalism is concerned you'll be a dead duck.'

'Take it easy, John.' Harry's attention was divided between Forest's voice and two papers on his writing table. One was the sheet of foolscap he had purloined in Starr's flat, and the other was a list which Inspector Munro had dictated to him a few minutes ago. 'The *Globe* will have full details in due course, but not yet. At the moment there's no story to tell.'

'No story? Then you must be mad – completely gaga.' Harry heard a newspaper rustle. 'According to the *Blast*'s evening edition, Starr went berserk. He shot a dog and a copper, kidnapped a child and barricaded himself in his flat. There was also a valuable collection of jewellery on the premises, and you think that isn't a story!'

'I said, not at the moment, John, and valuable is a mild adjective to describe what was found.' Harry picked up the list. 'The collection consists of the following items, so just listen and I'll read out the inventory.

' "One heavy, 17-carat gold chain with a sapphire pendant – four gold rings set with diamonds, pearls and Indian rubies – two silver bracelets and one silver crown or tiara, each embellished with a variety of important gem stones." ' He winced at the police clerk's pompous phraseology. ' "One round gold medallion with a fibula-type fastening, which was probably designed as a breast ornament. This medallion has a diameter of nine inches and a thickness of one-and-a-quarter inches. Its frontage bears a bas-relief depicting the Greek deity, Zeus, seducing the nymph, Leda, in the disguise of a swan. Three pearl necklaces, one diamond necklace." '

'An impressive hoard, isn't it?' Harry had come to the end of the list and he studied the second exhibit while he spoke. The paper was covered with pencilled lines, which appeared to show the interior of a building, and a marginal note seemed to confirm that that was the case: 'For your guidance, a rough plan of the location which our principal drew from memory.'

The letters were small and sprawling and Harry felt he would dislike the person who wrote them.

'Yes, Starr had a lot of loot in his flat, John, and Munro got Nathan Adler, the Bond Street dealer, to examine it. According to Adler the items range in date from the thirteenth to the seventeenth century, and the medallion could be the work of Benvenuto Cellini.'

'Cellini – the Renaissance goldsmith! Surely he was a hell of a big pot.' Forest was no longer angry and he gave a low whistle. 'But articles like that couldn't have been stolen from any ordinary collection. They're museum pieces, so where did Starr lift 'em? As far as I can remember there haven't been any thefts on that scale recently.'

'Your memory is quite correct and that's why there's no story for publication yet.' Harry was bent over the sketched plan. The drawing seemed to portray a large, domestic building – maybe a castle or a hall, and with luck it might be possible to pinpoint the actual place. 'Martin Starr worked with a brother and sister named Carlin and the three of them got hold of jewellery worth a king's ransom. But they didn't raid a museum or an art gallery. I'm almost certain of that. My guess is that the collection came from a private house, and I'm also pretty sure that very few people knew that it existed.'

'A hidden treasure – a king's ransom, eh.' Forest gloated over the terms. 'I like that, son. I like it very much indeed.'

'The treasure is only part of the business, John, and I want to write the full story for you.' Harry considered how much he should tell him. Certainly the interview in the confessional and his theft of the plan must be kept quiet – even Fatty Forest would frown on those actions. But he had to persuade Forest to give him *carte blanche.* He described Starr's death, he repeated what he had heard from Fergus Carlin, and he told him about Naureen's condition. When he finished he got what he wanted.

'Three tough villains are driven out of their wits by fear. Yes, I like that even more.' Harry could almost picture Forest licking his lips. 'You can follow the story through, my boy, and from this moment you are temporarily reinstated on the *Globe.*

I must however warn you on one point.' An unpleasant note returned to his voice. 'I gather that you didn't tell the police that there could be a connection between the deaths of Starr and this man, Carlin.

'No, I thought not, and that means you're guilty of withholding evidence, which is a pretty serious thing for a journalist to do. The *Looking Glass* was fined thirty thousand quid for it some years ago.

'This is what I propose Harry. You can draw any reasonable expenses, call on me if you want help, and take a week to get the complete story. But only a week, because the *Globe* has always enjoyed excellent relations with the police and those relations are going to continue.

'Providing you succeed within that time limit, you'll have your old job back, a substantial bonus, and my blessing.' There was the click of a switch and Harry realized that Forest was using an intercom and had taped their conversation. 'If you fail, however, Inspector Munro will be told everything you have just told me. Is that clear Harry?

'I said, is that clear?' Forest repeated the question loudly, but Harry hardly heard him, and all he could think about was the marginal note on the plan. He knew that he had seen such writing before and he not only disliked the man who penned it – he loathed him. Those small, sprawling letters had caused him a lot of eye-strain when he was ghosting the memoirs of Paul Trenton.

## Chapter 6

'You consider that Starr died because he had developed a pathological fear of rodents?' Miriam Stanford faced Harry across the same table in the hospital canteen. 'That the phobia was strong enough to stop his heart beating?'

'I don't just consider it, Miriam, I'm certain that's what happened. Starr didn't see a police-dog leaping through the window. He saw a gigantic rat and the sight of the creature killed him.' Harry had described Starr's death in detail and told her about the jewellery in the flat. 'I also suspect that something which happened during the robbery caused his phobia.'

'So you said, and until a few hours ago I would have thought you were insane yourself, and informed the police about my patient.' Miriam spoke quietly and she looked far less formidable than on their first meeting; younger and slightly forlorn. 'But now I am sure that if a third person questioned Naureen Carlin the shock would drive her completely insane and there'd be no hope of recovery.

'Thank you.' Harry had offered her a cigarette and this time she accepted. 'Naureen's physical symptoms, cramps and so forth, have returned and her system is not resisting them. Her mania returns as soon as she regains consciousness, and she screams and raves and tries to struggle off the bed. We're having to keep her sedated most of the time and that method of restraint can't continue indefinitely.' Miriam pulled at her cigarette. 'I'm completely out of my depth, but I think that the woman wants to die because she finds life unbearable.

'As you know, the tests and X-rays showed that there is no brain damage, and Starr's death seems to disprove my theory that the Carlins suffered from some inherited glandular complaint which only recurs at rare intervals.' She took another pull at the cigarette and frowned at him. 'I suppose the police surgeon checked that Starr had not been taking any drugs.'

'Very thoroughly. The police felt sure that must be the cause of his horrors, but there was nothing to suggest it.' Harry looked away from her. Bright morning sunlight flooded in through the canteen windows, but he had had a bad night and memories of the dark still troubled him. No monstrous snakes or rodents had disturbed his sleep after he'd spoken to Forest on the phone. The nightmare was based on the images of real events. A man's severed throat with the vocal cords exposed like scarlet sea anemones. A terrified child gasping for breath with a masked face peering behind her. Another man screaming at the approach of a dog. 'Starr and the Carlins shared a common experience which deranged them, Miriam.

Surely Naureen has given you some clue to what that experience could have been.'

'She's incapable of saying anything to help us, and so far we've been unable to help her. There's no response to E.C.T. or narco-analysis, no way to get through to the woman at all.' Miriam lowered her eyes as though the admissions of failure were embarrassing her. 'If this was the African jungle or we were living in the Middle Ages, I'd say that someone had put a curse on Naureen Carlin and the spell was destroying her – rotting her body and soul and mind.'

'Perhaps someone has.' Harry stubbed out his cigarette and felt the envelope containing the sketched plan crinkle in his pocket. 'It seems likely that a fourth person may have been involved in this robbery. An ex-doctor named Trenton.'

'Paul Trenton!' Miriam looked up with a jerk. 'The man who was struck off the register for negligence?'

'The same.' Harry spoke savagely. 'Trenton knew Martin Starr. There was a note in his handwriting in Starr's flat and if I can find him and get him to talk, I might . . .' He broke off and stared at Miriam's expression. 'You know the man?'

'Only slightly. We could be described as professional rivals, and I lost a patient because of him.' It was Miriam's turn to express bitterness. 'A year ago Susan Vallance, the actress, consulted me about a nervous complaint that was troubling her and I started treatment. Only started, though. On my third visit to her flat Trenton was there and Susan told me that she no longer required psychiatric help, and he was going to give her a course of massage. She was very pleasant about it, but I was naturally angry. Also concerned, because she needed analysis badly and massage was quite useless. I think that she might not have flopped in *Saint Joan* without Trenton's intervention.'

'That's very possible.' Harry remembered how nonchalantly Paul Trenton had strolled away from the theatre. 'Doc Trenton enjoys hurting people, Miriam. Destruction is his hobby, and he might easily have made Miss Vallance feel that she was doomed to failure.'

'I don't understand you.' Miriam raised her eyebrows. 'I didn't care for the man, and I was resentful at the time, but he didn't strike me as being at all sinister; merely misguided and bumptious.'

'He is sinister, Miriam, and I'm one of the few people who know just how sinister.' Harry finished his coffee. 'And thank you for the information. After the *Saint Joan* affair I don't suppose Miss Vallance is still receiving treatment from him, but she might have his address.'

'Almost certainly, though I don't think she'll give it to anybody without asking Trenton's permission. Susan Vallance is a great believer in personal privacy.' Miriam was frowning at his expression. 'You've obviously got a bee in your bonnet about Trenton, Harry. He was an incompetent surgeon, but I can't imagine him being involved in a robbery. He's not a common crook.'

'No, not a common one. Paul Trenton's criminal activities are most uncommon, and I must find out where he lives.' A course of action was forming in Harry's mind. A link between Trenton and Starr had been established and there might be other links at the Doc's residence. When he knew that address he intended to turn his own hand to burglary. 'Please ask Miss Vallance, Miriam.'

'You really believe that Trenton may somehow be responsible for these people's illnesses?' Miriam was still frowning at him. 'Very well, Harry, I'll see what I can do.'

'Thank you, Miriam, but it is also important that I get the address without Trenton knowing anyone is interested in it.' His eyes pleaded with her. 'Will you do that for me?'

'No, because I've just thought of a better idea.' She took a final drag at her cigarette. 'There is a good chance that I may see Trenton myself this evening, and no reason why you shouldn't be present at our meeting.'

Forest had allowed him a week, the first day was drawing to a close and it had been an exhausting and alcoholic one. Though Harry was late for his appointment, he drove slowly through the rush-hour traffic. He had high hopes that the scheme he and Miriam had discussed would work and he was on his way to a party. A very distinguished party given by Dame Susan Vallance to toast the success of her forthcoming play, *Our Lady of Pain*. Miriam was invited and she had asked Miss Vallance if she might bring a friend. The actress had graciously consented, and if Trenton was also a guest, the wolf would be closing in on the sleigh.

But Harry's other hopes had not been fulfilled. He'd believed that the plan he'd taken from Starr's flat might help him locate the scene of the robbery, but there was no joy on that score. Because Starr and the Carlins had never worked abroad, it seemed likely that the building was somewhere in the British Isles, but that could be anywhere from Land's End to John-o-'Groat's. As Trenton's note stated, the thing was just a rough sketch, intended as a general guide to the layout, and the experts he'd consulted had been unable to help. Mr Vincent Rammage, the editor of *House and Homestead*, could offer no suggestion – Dr Lambert of the Whitehall Topographical Society equally perplexed – Professor the Honourable Sir Hector Brigham-Beer, Curator of the National Heritage Museum, downright rude.

'Yes, Mister . . . Mister . . . er . . . Clay, I am an authority in the field of domestic architecture; probably the only authority worth bothering about, and as you doubtless know, my published works – *Fortified Manor Houses* – *The Seats of the English Nobility and Landed Gentry* – *Sewage Disposal in Tudor Times*, are standard text books in most universities.

'However, Mister . . . Mr Clay, though I am a savant and a man of letters, I am not God.' Sir Hector was a lordly person and he raised a hand as if expecting Harry to accuse him of false modesty.

'Your newspaper bought a collection of manuscripts from the widow of Edgar Mayne, the celebrated ghost hunter, and you hope to do an article on haunted houses.' The professor had swallowed Harry's story and been eager to help at first, but his patience was short-lived. 'Among Mayne's papers you found this childish scrawl and expect me to identify the actual building.' Harry had given him a photostat of the paper, which did not show the marginal note, and he held it to the light and snorted loudly. 'An impossible task, even for an expert such as myself.

'As you can see, only the ground-floor interior is shown and that is not drawn to scale. Just look at this corridor – it's wider than the rooms leading off from it. And as for these walls, which are presumably intended to support the roof . . . Pshaw!' Harry had never heard the archaic expression actually voiced before, and Brigham-Beer followed it with a sound that was part groan and part sigh.

'This is just a doodle, such as an idle person might scribble on a telephone directory, and the person in question is an ig- noramus. He has no knowledge of architecture, engineering principles, or technical drawing. If any structure was based on this creation it would have crashed to the ground centuries ago.

'Oh yes, it is supposed to show an old, or oldish building, Mr Clay.' He squinted at the photograph as though it were a highly indecent piece of graffiti. 'The main block and two of the wings are late Elizabethan or early Jacobean in style, and an additional wing was added around the middle of the last century. At a guess I would say that this – this – ' He was at a loss to express his contempt. 'This thing is an attempt to por- tray a medium-sized country mansion rather than a large town house, but such idle conjecture is worthless.

'In fact you are wasting my time, Mr Clay, and that is a very valuable commodity.' He pointed at the door with a gesture that made Harry think of an eastern potentate dismissing one of his least touchable subjects.

No help from Starr's plan and no help from the police, though Inspector Munro was grateful to Harry and had told him all he knew. The jewellery appeared to be unique and none of the items had been reported stolen from any museum, pri- vate collection or shop. Munro's personal theory was the same as the one which had delighted John Forest. In the inspector's

view, no actual burglary was involved and Starr and his confederates had somehow stumbled on a treasure trove. A cache
that had been hidden away and lain forgotten for centuries.

No help from the underworld either. After leaving Munro,
Harry had visited a number of shady clubs and public houses
which Starr and the Carlins sometimes frequented. He had
heard plenty of comment about the two deaths, and much
curiosity as to why a hard case like 'good old Marty' should
have gone off his rocker. It was also known that Fergus Carlin
had had the shakes shortly before his death, but that was all.
Nobody knew any details about the gang's last job or who had
organized it.

Seven o'clock. Harry looked at his watch as he stopped
the car before a traffic signal. He had to attend that party, because there was a chance that Trenton might also be a guest,
but he wasn't looking forward to it. He'd drunk far too much
during his search for information, his eyes smarted behind
their lenses, his mouth felt stale, and remorse was troubling
him. He'd impersonated a priest, he'd stolen evidence from
the police and he was just as bad as the people he'd recently
talked to. Vicious, loud-mouthed people on the way up talking
about flashy cars and flashy women, horse racing and property
deals. Vicious, furtive people who smiled pleasantly, but said
very little. Vicious, abject people who'd fallen into the gutter
and would never climb out of it.

Not at all the kind of people Susan Vallance would be enter-
taining, though many of those might be equally vicious; especially vicious where their hostess was concerned, and they had
reason to be. Not long ago Harry had attended a civic reception at which Dame Susan was the guest of honour and he'd
witnessed the reason for her unpopularity. Though openly
courteous, her manner had been so superior that he'd almost
felt pleased that *Saint Joan* had flopped.

But flop or no flop, Miss Vallance obviously lived in style.
The lights had changed to green, Harry turned a corner and
his goal was in sight. Lethbridge Mansions, an imposing block
of flats, with a uniformed porter at the entrance, large, well-

polished cars in the forecourt, and balconies and bay windows proclaiming money. And more than money. Behind the marble faced walls were very select residences and one couldn't buy a lease by merely producing a cheque book.

Harry parked his ageing Ford between a Rolls and a Mercedes, reversing into the gap so that its bonnet was facing the exit in case a quick departure was needed. If Trenton was at the party, he intended to follow him when he left, and the man might hail another passing taxi.

Trenton will be at the party, he reassured himself, as he climbed out of the car and a cold breeze revived his spirits and cleared his brain. Trenton is the prime mover, the one person who knows what drove those people mad and where they stole the treasure. His feet dragged slightly as he approached the entrance, the porter eyed his off-the-peg suit with disapproval, but Harry hardly noticed him. He had drawn a lot of blanks, he had committed two serious misdemeanours, but so what? He was a journalist – a reporter with a story to write.

Yes, a story. His confidence returned at every step, and he grinned when he reached the lift and pressed a button. A story – the scoop of a ruddy lifetime.

# Chapter 7

An earl and a cabinet minister and a millionaire – a best-selling novelist and two film stars – a peeress and a world-famous portrait painter. The elite were well-represented at Miss Vallance's soirée, but plenty of smaller fry were also present. The actress prided herself on having a large and varied circle of acquaintances and over a hundred people were gathered in her sitting-room. One of them was Paul Trenton.

'I was commissioned to write the play for Susan, and with all modesty I think I can say that my labours have borne impressive fruit.' Miriam had been waiting near the door for Harry, but soon after his arrival their hostess had beckoned her away and he was lumbered with an acquaintance he had met at the Press Club from time to time. Patricia Nevern, the dramatist responsible for *Our Lady of Pain.*

'To portray Elizabeth of Hungary as a heroine took some doing I can tell you, Clay.' Miss Nevern was a large, talkative woman with a masculine manner and a craggy weatherbeaten face that made Harry think of a boxer – a boxer dog. 'I had the devil of a job making her a sympathetic character.'

'Why shouldn't her character be sympathetic?' Harry spoke out of politeness, because he found Miss Nevern a crashing bore. He'd wanted to talk to Miriam about Naureen Carlin and he wanted to watch Trenton. The Doc was not in a sociable mood. He stood alone in a corner and declined coldly whenever the hired waiter or one of the two resident maids offered to refill his empty glass. His eyes were riveted on Miss Vallance and there was a small black bag at his feet.

'What a damn silly question to ask, Clay.' The dramatist raised a pair of prominent eyebrows which were tinted purple to match the colour of her mannishly-cut dress. 'If you consider the career of Hungarian Liz, you must realize what a sweat it was.' She nodded across to Dame Susan, who was standing before a big oil painting with Miriam and the artist, Oswald Kerr, at her side. 'I was furious when I heard that Susan had persuaded Ossie to paint her in the role, because I can't stand him. But I have to admit that he's caught the Lady's aura a treat.'

'It is certainly striking.' Harry nodded. The picture was almost life-size and showed a tall woman turning her face away from a window. Her hands were clasped as if in prayer, rays of light mottled her long, white robe like bloodstains or scarlet flames, and there was a gold crown on her head. The sitter could have been Susan Vallance, though the face on the canvas was broader and had high Slavonic cheekbones. Its features were set in a grimace which suggested almost animal ferocity.

'Ah, thank you, Betty.' Miss Nevern ogled the maid as she poured them more champagne and then raised her glass. 'Cheers, Clay, and down with the drink.'

'Cheers.' Harry followed suit unwillingly. He'd drunk four

or five whiskies in the clubs, three pints of beer in the public houses, and Miss Vallance's champagne was liberally laced with brandy.

'The picture shows the opening scene of my play, which is a flashback.' Miss Nevern eyed the painting as though it was her own creation. 'When the curtain rises the stage is in complete darkness and then a light appears at the window to reveal Susan's profile and produce the usual cliché of the rising sun. But it's not sunrise, my boy.' She paused impressively. 'The light comes from a three thousand candle-power arc lamp controlled by a dimmer switch. For a full minute and a half Susan stands motionless while the beam becomes brighter and brighter, and then – Wow.' Miss Nevern slapped her thigh. 'Susan suddenly screams at the top of her voice and swings away from the window to face the auditorium. At the same instant the lamp is banged on to full power and you get the effect of Elizabeth burning in hell-fire.

'Should rock the audience in their seats, and very exact timing is needed, because that lamp's second cousin to a small searchlight. Before she turns away, Susan's face is only three feet from the lens.'

'A pretty dangerous stunt.' Harry considered the feelings their hostess aroused in subordinates. 'What would happen if the timing went wrong? If there was a short in the circuit, or the switch-operator made a mistake?' He glanced at Trenton while he spoke. The man was still alone and he had not even noticed him because he seemed to have eyes for nothing except Susan Vallance. 'Couldn't the light blind her?'

'It most certainly could, Clay. She'd probably be knocked cold. Might fall forward and burn her face on the carbons.' Miss Nevern spoke with relish. 'But accidents like that rarely happen in the theatre these days, and the gimmick was Dame Bighead's idea, not mine. Susan wanted the play to start with a real bang and damned nearly dictated how the scene should be written. The story of Elizabeth has been a sort of fetish for her over the years, and that's why she made such a hash of *Saint Joan*, in my opinion. If God's gift to drama wants to go the whole hog and risk her sight, I can't stop her. Remember what she said when the audience slow-handclapped her after the Shaw flop. "You do not like me as a saint, and I bow to your judgment." ' She imitated the actress's throbbing, contralto voice. ' "But when you next see me I shall play a demon and tear your souls." '

'Yes, I do remember hearing that, but I'm still not with you about the plot, Miss Nevern.' Harry saw that Trenton was looking in their direction, but there was no hint of recognition in his face. 'Wasn't Elizabeth of Hungary a saint? A pious queen who gave so much food away to the poor her family went short. Annoying for the family, but hardly diabolical.'

'Good grief! We're talking at cross-purposes and you've got the wrong Lizzie. The play's about Elizabeth Bathori, of course – the Countess of Nadasdy.' Harry's expression had remained blank and the purple eyebrows were raised again. 'Dear me, you really are an ignoramus, Clay.'

'While you are a most incompetent mimic, Patricia.' Miss Vallance and Miriam had crossed over to them. Dame Susan had heard the imitation, and though her tone was good-humoured on the surface, her eyes were furious. Rather tired eyes surrounded by crow's feet that her make-up didn't quite hide. Nor did it hide the thin white line above her left cheek. The mark of a razor that some anonymous ill-wisher had planted in a stick of grease-paint.

'You can also be rather a stupid old bitch at times, Patricia, though you're right to say that Mr Clay is badly informed for a theatre critic.' She had obviously read Harry's fictitious notice of *Saint Joan* and bowed mockingly. 'I shall be pleased to give you the information about the character I am playing, Mr Clay, but first we must all have another drink.

'Over here, Betty.' She motioned to the maid and Harry winced at the prospect of more champagne. For some reason Trenton seemed worried too and there was a frown on his face while their glasses were refilled.

'Elizabeth Bathori was the niece of King Stephen of Poland, and widow of a Hungarian count named Nadasdy. It is pre-

sumed – supposed – thought – that she died in the early years
of the seventeenth century.' Miss Vallance's voice had a hyp-
notic quality and several nearby guests stopped talking to listen
to her.

'For many years before Elizabeth's supposed death, the
Hungarian authorities became concerned by the disappearance of a large number of peasant girls in the area around
Castle Nadasdy. After a while a rumour spread that the countess and her sister and their servants were responsible for these
disappearances.' Miss Nevern was correct in saying that Susan
Vallance was obsessed with the story and her words flowed
out as dramatically as though she was on the stage. 'But no
action was taken, Mr Clay – nothing was done for a long
time, because another rumour had spread.' Over her shoulder
Harry saw that Paul Trenton's frown had deepened and he was
licking his lower lip. 'People said that the countess possessed
rather peculiar powers and it was unwise to thwart her.

'Superstitious nonsense, Mr Clay? A fairy tale to frighten
children?' She spoke more quietly, but her enthusiasm was as
apparent as a physical presence – as the smell of fear that had
come from Marty Starr and Fergus Carlin. And not only enthusiasm – anxiety was present as well. Dame Susan was like
a mountaineer preparing to risk her life on the crucial pitch of
an unclimbed peak.

'But when girls of noble birth as well as peasants started to
disappear, action had to be taken, and one night soldiers entered the castle. The countess's sister was not at home, but she
herself was overpowered in her bedchamber before she could
light a candle or call for help and her face was blindfolded. She
and all the members of her household were then put to the
torture, and after a while one of her maids talked and led the
soldiers down to the castle vaults.

'How Elizabeth pleaded with her companions to keep
silent! Though masked and stretched out on the rack her own
spirit could not be broken and she struggled to inspire them.
"What is pain to us who have drunk the waters of eternity and
are sealed by His grace?"' Miss Vallance was clearly quoting

from the script and the whole room had fallen silent. ' "What is physical suffering compared to the joys we have shared together, and will share again?" ' Her face had turned to the big oil painting and Miriam and Harry saw that there was a nervous tic trembling beside the scar. ' "Fear nothing, my friends, for I am Elizabeth Bathori, the niece of a king and the hands of men cannot kill me. I am your mistress and your mother, your protector and your lover and I order you to ignore pain and hold your tongue." '

'Very . . . er . . . dramatic, Susan darling.' She had come to the end of the speech and the peeress interposed, hesitating over the adjective to show that, in her view, melodramatic might be a better description. 'But please do continue. We are all agog to know what was found in the vaults and what your countess's powers were.'

'Then go and see the bleedin' play, ducks. It opens termorrer, don't it?' Miss Vallance adopted a pert cockney accent. 'And I'll need a good nite's sleep, won't I? So, sorry, boys and girls, it's bin luvely 'avin yer, but the party's over.' She was a better mimic than the playwright and her dismissal was greeted by chuckles and the obedient emptying of glasses.

But Harry did not chuckle and neither did Paul Trenton. During Dame Susan's performance, Trenton had picked up his bag and sidled quietly out of the room, and without using physical violence against a woman Harry was unable to follow him. As he started for the door a powerful hand tugged at his jacket and a voice boomed in his ear. 'What's the rush, Clay? I want to ask you something.' Two questions were involved. Had he a car – was he going anywhere near Earl's Court? Simple inquiries, but by the time Harry had answered them and the hand released him, it was too late.

Patricia Nevern got a lift – Doc Trenton got away.

# Chapter 8

'In the castle vaults they found the mutilated bodies of six hundred and fifty girls.' Patricia Nevern continued the story in the car, but Harry's thoughts were on Paul Trenton. Once again Trenton had eluded him and Miss Vallance had coldly refused to tell Miriam where the man lived. He felt angry, frustrated and ashamed of himself.

'Yes, over six hundred, Dr Stanford. A most creditable figure even for those stirring times.' Miss Nevern looked even more mannish in a military-type greatcoat with brass buttons and the epaulets of a Victorian major-general on the shoulders. 'The countess's score card puts Bluebeard in the second division and it was she, not Dracula, who originated the vampire legend.

'Elizabeth Bathori appeared to have founded a sort of Manson-type hippie group and her victims had all been ritually tortured before death, which was achieved by hanging them head down from the cellar ceiling and slitting their throats.' The dramatist lolled sideways in the back seat with her legs stretched across the car. 'Sadism and lesbianism were definitely involved, witchcraft probably was, but the main motivation for the murders was medical. Lizzie and her sister believed that fresh human blood could stave off old age, and the children provided them with living shower baths.'

'Susan Vallance told me that her part was romantic.' Miriam was in the front beside Harry and she looked round with a frown. 'It must have been difficult to make romance out of mania, perversion and mass murder, Miss Nevern.'

'Damn difficult, my dear, but I'm a damn good writer.' She beamed proudly. 'I used the same technique that Milton did in *Paradise Lost*. You may disapprove of the Miltonian concept of a noble Satan: Lucifer, the Fallen Star of the Morning, but there's no denying that he's impressive. Makes God appear a fuddle-de-dee at times.

'That's what I've done with the countess and I just hope that Susan has enough self-control to give the role realism. The neurotic bitch has been terribly edgy during rehearsals and I'm keeping my fingers crossed that she'll come up with the lights.'

*Up with the lights.* Harry knew that the phrase was a common theatrical expression for a play's first performance, but it made him think of a particular light. The second cousin to a small searchlight that could stun and blind. A vague notion was running through his mind, but it wouldn't take logical form and he cursed the drinks that he'd had. 'What's making her edgy? Anxiety that she may have another flop like *Saint Joan*?'

'That's part of it, but there's a good deal more. And do watch your driving, Clay, because you're making me edgy too.' Harry had almost scraped a taxi and Miss Nevern sat upright with a jerk. 'Susan is obsessed with the character – schizophrenically obsessed in my view – and tends to overact. She's also worried about her appearance, and rightly so. As Ossie's painting shows so well, the countess should have heavy, almost masculine features, and Susan is a very feminine creature. We tried filling out her cheeks with pads, but that ruined her voice so one must hope for the best. She's blindfolded during the trial scene which is the crux of the play, so her appearance may not be too much of a drawback.

'And a bloody marvellous trial scene it is, though I say so myself.' She beamed again. 'Justifies all the tiresome research that was needed. I had to brush up my foreign languages for that. Apart from Baring-Gould's *Book of Werewolves* there are comparatively few accounts of the case in English.'

'You mean the play is based on an actual story?' Miriam shared Harry's ignorance. 'Those murders were actually committed?'

'Good heavens, yes. My poetic imagination embellished history here and there, but the script contains all the main facts and nobody can question the fictional additions. The Bathori family were extremely influential and they persuaded the Hungarian authorities to hush the matter up as much as possible.

'But though most of the data were handed down by word of mouth like the Norse sagas, it is quite definite that Lizzie and her cronies kidnapped, tortured and killed those girls and they paid for their fun.' Miss Nevern spoke with the same relish as when she had mentioned the possibility that Susan Vallance might be injured by the arc lamp. 'Elizabeth's sister, Krisia – inappropriately enough that is the Polish pet name version of Christine – was not at the castle when the soldiers arrived and she fled the country and was never heard of again. But the rest of the group came to very sticky ends. Some were burned as witches, some impaled on stakes, others disembowelled while they were still alive. Painful ways to die, though nothing compared to the countess's fate. She suffered the worst punishment of all.'

The worst punishment – the worst fate – the worst thing in the world – a revulsion that varies from individual to individual. The phrases rang through Harry's blurred brain. The horror that had haunted Carlin and Starr – that was probably still torturing Naureen Carlin. 'How did they execute the countess?'

'They didn't execute her, Clay. Elizabeth Bathori was the niece of a former king of Poland, and custom forbade the shedding of royal blood. She was allowed to live.

'After a fashion, that is.' Miss Nevern wound down a window and smiled at the lighted shop fronts. 'It's nice to breathe fresh air, and nice to look at the lights, isn't it? The last light poor Lizzie saw was on the evening before her arrest. The last fresh air she breathed was outside the fortress of a town called Csej.

'This will do me splendidly, Clay, so please pull over to the kerb and I'll try to finish the yarn before a copper moves you on.

'They walled up Lizzie Bathori in a *little ease*. A tiny egg-shaped cell in which she could neither stand nor sit nor lie down. A hole in the floor served her as a privy, she obtained water by licking the damp walls, food was passed to her through a hatch so that she could not see or be seen by her jailors.' Harry had stopped the car and Miss Nevern opened a door.

'Not an enviable existence. No light – no sound – no sensation except discomfort. The stench of your body – your back bent like a hoop – your tongue scraping against stone in search of moisture. How long would a human being survive in such conditions, Dr Stanford?'

'A few days, I suppose.' Miriam felt slightly sick because the playwright was clearly revelling in the gruesome details. 'A week or two at the most.'

'I bow to your professional knowledge, my dear.' Patricia Nevern smiled as she climbed out of the car. 'And your answer implies that people could have been right about the Bathori sisters. Maybe they did possess rather peculiar powers.

'No, it would spoil your enjoyment of the play if I went into details.' Miriam had questioned her, but she shook her head and turned to Harry. 'I'm sure that Dr Stanford is a most competent medical practitioner, Clay, and she is right in saying that a normal human being could only endure the countess's agony for a brief period of time. But this is a historical fact.' She buttoned up her coat, the general's epaulets gleaming under a street lamp.

'Elizabeth Bathori was buried alive in 1610. She was still alive almost four years later.'

'Thank you, Sister.' After Miss Nevern left them, Harry and Miriam had gone to his flat and she was calling the hospital. 'Yes, I'll see her first thing in the morning, naturally.' Miriam replaced the telephone and sighed. 'Naureen Carlin's temperature is now 103°, Harry. The sedatives are sapping her resistance, but without them those imaginary fears will kill her.' She sat down facing him. 'Your objectionable dramatist friend may be right about the countess's powers of survival, but Naureen isn't surviving her agony. The mind is destroying the body and she's sinking. Could be dead in a day or two.'

'And die without revealing what caused her fears – without telling you what she and Fergus and Martin Starr did – what

Doc Trenton made them do?' Harry had had two cups of black coffee, but his mind was still hazy and he had difficulty in marshalling his thoughts. 'Patricia Nevern is no friend of mine, Miriam. I only know her slightly and she's a bloody nuisance. Without her I could have followed Trenton and found out where he lived.'

'With a view to breaking into his premises, I suppose.' Miriam spoke coldly. 'I admit that I don't like Trenton, Harry. His negligence made two people suffer and I resented Susan Vallance preferring his treatment to mine. But I'm sure what you suggested on our way here can't be true.'

'Can't it?' Harry struggled to express his half-formed theories. 'Those jewels were probably stolen from a country house, but more than robbery may have been involved. Though Fergus Carlin was rambling in the pub he seemed to imply that Naureen might have knifed a child. No case of child wounding has been reported recently, so isn't murder or abduction possible? The parents may think the kid is staying with friends or relatives. The hosts that it's gone home.' Harry stood up and paced the floor in the hope that movement would help him concentrate. 'If that is true, Naureen did something quite contrary to her normal moral code and intense guilt might account for her condition.'

'Not in my opinion.' Miriam shook her head impatiently. 'Three people were involved, remember, and I can't see guilt affecting them all to such an extent. And why should they commit a crime that was repugnant to their natural instincts, Harry?'

'Dope, Miriam.' He lit a cigarette and inhaled deeply. 'I know that none of the gang were addicts and no trace of drugs was found in their bloodstreams. But isn't it feasible that there could be a substance which doesn't reveal its presence? A chemical similar to L.S.D., acting on the imagination. A hallucinogenic which first deadens guilt and then multiplies it by turning commonplace dislikes into unbearable revulsions?'

'If so, it's a substance that I've never heard of, Harry, and they'd have found evidence of L.S.D. Lysergic acid leaves what is known as a *pink spot* in the urine, and its effects would have worn off by now. Naureen was admitted to hospital yesterday afternoon.' Miriam occasionally visited a clinic for juvenile delinquents and she adopted a tone reserved for the more truculent cases. 'Because there may be a link between Starr and Paul Trenton, you've got it into your head that Trenton is the mad scientist of fiction. The inventor of a mysterious drug that is quite untraceable and continues to act after leaving the system.

'I said I didn't care for Trenton, Harry, but your notion is too off-beat for words. The man is a surgeon, not a chemist, so how did he produce this miraculous substance which is quite unknown to medicine to the best of my knowledge? How did he administer it to the gang and what possible motive could he have had?'

'I can't answer your first questions, but as to motive . . .' Harry dragged at his cigarette again and stared at the drifting smoke as though it might form words to solve the problem. 'Trenton could have wanted Starr and the Carlins to commit a crime that they would never have considered unless they were under the influence of drugs. It is also possible that they were chosen at random. Guinea-pigs to test his product before it was given to more important victims.'

'You're talking in riddles, Harry.' Miriam's tone became even more brusque. 'What victims?'

'Miss Vallance may be one of them. Patricia Nevern told us how edgy she's been during rehearsals and she was on tenterhooks this evening. Remember how she suddenly broke up the party.'

'What's strange about that? The play opens tomorrow, and of course Susan is tense. Another flop like *Saint Joan* would ruin her and she'd become a has-been with a lot of former friends sniggering behind their crocodile tears.'

'Exactly. So isn't it likely that she might be glad if someone offered to help her get through the first night?' Harry crossed to his desk. 'Can't you hear her thanking the donor – and picture the pleasure in his face as he obliges. An injection or a pep pill with a price tag attached to it. A killer that first lifts you up and then destroys you.' He clutched the desk top to steady himself. 'Hell, you've seen Naureen Carlin, and I don't have to describe the symptoms.'

'I can also see you, Harry, and you're drunk and talking nonsense.' Miriam's irritation increased. 'You're suggesting that Trenton wishes to harm Susan Vallance, but you have no motive to offer.'

'Yes I have, though you may not believe me. The police didn't think much of my story at the time.' Harry opened a drawer. 'You're a psychologist, Miriam, and you probably consider that all mental illness has a logical cause and effect. That a man who attacks middle-aged women must have been maltreated by his mother, for instance. But I've got a notion that certain people are possessed by forces which have nothing to do with environment or heredity. That they are driven to hurt and destroy because destruction is the force which controls them.

'That sounds crazy, doesn't it, and as you've said I am tight. I can't express myself clearly, but perhaps these will give you some idea what makes Trenton tick.' Harry took five photographs from the drawer and walked back to her holding out four of them. 'The Countess of Seaford and Mrs Marjorie Carlton before and after treatment by Dr Paul Trenton F.R.C.S.'

'I've seen these before.' She glanced briefly at the pictures and handed them back. 'Trenton's case was fully reported in the *English Medical Journal*. Those women were disfigured because of his negligence but that doesn't make him a criminal psychopath.'

'But I rather think the last exhibit does.' Harry laid the fifth photograph on the arm of her chair and Miriam's irritation vanished. She picked the print up and shuddered.

'Not very pretty, is it?' Harry said. 'The girl's name was Violet Frome and she was a prostitute before that was done to her. I don't suppose she gets much custom nowadays.'

'She's not only scarred, Harry. She's been blinded.' Miriam had to force herself to keep looking at the ravaged face. 'Was it acid?'

'Yes, sulphuric administered shortly before I started ghost-writing Trenton's memoirs.' He took the picture from her. 'Miss Frome picked up a client in the course of business one afternoon and took him to her room. The man seemed normal enough and she was completely off her guard when he came up behind her with a chloroform pad. After regaining consciousness she was naturally in no state to describe her attacker.'

'I could do with a drink myself, Harry.' Miriam had believed that no human wickedness could surprise her, but the picture had left her weak and shaken. 'Brandy if you have it.'

'Of course.' Harry went over to the sideboard. 'A few days later Miss Frome told the police that the man had appeared quite nondescript; middle-aged, middle-class, quietly dressed. There was no outstanding physical characteristic she could remember, though he had said his name was Savage – Edward Savage.' Harry came back with the brandy. 'A pseudonym of course, and the police never had a suspect. It probably wouldn't have done them much good if they had. How could poor, blind Violet Frome identify anybody?'

'And you think that the man was Trenton?' Miriam took a deep drink of brandy. 'Why, Harry?'

'One day while I was working with Trenton on the memoirs, a copy of that picture happened to be on my office table. I was called away for a moment or two and when I got back he didn't hear me enter the room and he didn't see me either. All Trenton could see was the photograph and he was grinning at it. Grinning and rubbing his hands together and I knew that that monstrosity was his own handiwork. Though the police didn't believe me I am absolutely certain that Doc Trenton and Edward Savage are the same man.'

'He was rubbing his hands together this evening, Harry.' Miriam finished the drink and stood up. 'He also kept staring at Susan Vallance. He couldn't take his eyes off her.' Miriam opened her handbag and as she did, she remembered another bag. A black leather bag beside a man's foot – perhaps a medical bag. She also remembered what Patricia Nevern had said about Dame Susan's appearance and the attempts to fill out her cheeks with pads.

'Susan is obsessed with the role, Harry. I think she'd go to any lengths to ensure the success of the play, and if you're right about Trenton, something horrible could happen tomorrow night. He may not have left the flat after the party, but waited in another room till the last guests had gone.' Miriam consulted her memo book and hurried to the phone with images running through her head. A hypodermic needle forcing petroleum jelly between bone and flesh to make a thin, feminine face stronger and more masculine. A woman standing before a stage window. An arc lamp which glowed dimly at first to produce the illusion of sunrise and then brighter and brighter. The heat of the carbons and the power of the beam increasing till they were intolerable to bear. Before that happened Susan Vallance had to turn away quickly, but the damage might have been done before she turned. Miriam dialled a number and considered the final image.

Miss Nevern hoped that the audience would be shaken when Susan Vallance swung round and screamed, but it might not be the dramatic effect that moved them. They might be horrified by a pathetic monstrosity.

If Trenton had injected petroleum jelly – if the jelly was not of the correct consistency – if the lamp had melted it before she turned, Miss Vallance's face would be a sagging, deformed caricature of her former beauty.


## Chapter 9

'I am not insane, Miriam, but I suspect that you may be and all I can say is "Physician, heal thyself."' Miss Vallance stood before the big oil painting of Elizabeth Bathori. She was dressed exactly the same as the woman in the picture, with a long, white robe, a crown on her head, and her feet were sandalled. One of her maids had led her into the room when Harry and

Miriam arrived and she still held the girl's arm. There was a glaringly red bandage across her eyes.

'You and Mr Clay honestly thought I would be rash enough to let Paul Trenton perform plastic surgery on me when I open tomorrow night.' With the eyes concealed her face was expressionless but she spoke with regal arrogance and the personal pronoun revealed her character. She had not said 'when the play opens', or 'when we open', but 'when I open'. As far as the great lady was concerned the rest of the cast were puppets to support her performance.

'Trenton is no longer a member of your lofty profession, Miriam, but he has something you lack – the gift of healing.' Her mouth curved into a smile as though she could see through the bandage and had noticed Miriam flush. 'He has been giving me a course of massage for some months now and the headaches I used to suffer from hardly trouble me at all. At every session his hands have done me more good than the weary hours I spent discussing my nerves with you.

'I wanted a final tone-up for tomorrow and that is why Trenton stayed behind after the party. He left a few minutes ago and I was feeling the benefits of his labours till your untimely arrival disturbed me.

'And it is now time for your departure.' She let go of the maid and gave a gesture that reminded Harry of the obnoxious Professor Brigham-Beer. 'Please show them out, Jean.'

'We are not leaving without an explanation, Susan.' Miriam stared at the strip of red cloth. She had been anxious when she'd lifted the phone and learned that Miss Vallance was with Paul Trenton and could not be disturbed, and her anxiety had increased as they hurried to Harry's car and drove off through the thin late-evening traffic. But anxiety had turned to horror when she saw that bandaged face and for a moment she'd felt sure that a major operation had been performed and blood was staining the material. That fear was over now, because Dame Susan seemed to be in robust health. No incision could have been made, and there was no change in the woman's visible features. Trenton had not used wax or jelly to alter her appearance, but the bandage must be there for a purpose. Might it conceal a row of tiny stitches inserted to tauten the ageing cheek muscles? Such stitches could have been made quickly and painlessly under a local anaesthetic and grease paint would hide them. But one of Trenton's former patients had received the same treatment from him and infection followed. If his needle had not been sterilized Miss Vallance might be feeling very ill before long and the opening curtain would rise on her understudy.

'Trenton obviously did something to your face, Susan, and we are not going till you remove the bandage and let me examine you.'

'Damn your impertinence.' It was the actress's turn to flush and she waved the maid aside. 'You had better leave us, Jean.' She waited till the girl had closed the door behind her and then her mouth curled again. 'Please forgive me, Miriam dear. One shouldn't be rude to guests in front of servants, should one? Even unwanted guests.'

'We're still waiting.' Miss Vallance had the knack of making an apology sound far ruder than the original insult, but Miriam was too concerned to be angry. 'Why are you wearing that bandage?'

'Simply because I am an actress with a part to practise.' Arrogance gave way to resignation and she shrugged. 'Very well. As you demand to be enlightened I must enlighten you.

'Will one of you please lead me across the hall and through the second doorway on the right.' She gripped Harry's arm tightly and let him guide her forward, planting her feet with care as if fearing a fall.

'I can manage on my own now.' They had entered a large bedroom and she released her grasp. 'The last act of the play is a trial scene, and though I am the prisoner I am allowed to move about the court and confront my accusers and the judges. But I am in no way a free agent because my wrists are chained and my eyes blindfolded. Do you understand now?'

'I'm beginning to.' Miriam looked at the furniture which was moved away from the walls as though decorators were due to start work. Two beds were set head-to-middle to form a 'T', a dressing-table and a tallboy stood at right-angles to each other, and chairs and chests of drawers had been placed in unusual positions. 'This is a sort of mock-up of the stage set?'

'Of course.' Miss Vallance moved across to a rectangle of chairs. 'I am now standing inside the dock, the beds represent the witness box and the tallboy and dressing-table are the judges' bench.' She placed her hands behind her back to give the impression that they were shackled and walked around the room, moving so confidently and gracefully that Miriam and Harry almost suspected that she could see through the cloth. 'I have not merely to be word-perfect for the part. My feet must know exactly where they are going. Is the mystery solved, Miriam?'

'Not entirely. I would have thought a bandage with slits or holes which were invisible to the audience would have done just as well.'

'I'm sure you do and that is the prop a less meticulous artist would use.' Miss Vallance's robe swept the carpet as she returned to the chairs. 'But whenever possible I try to live my roles and I want to share Elizabeth Bathori's experiences. To feel as she must have felt at the time. The recurring theme of the play is based on colour and the lack of colour. Lamplight and the glistening redness of blood – the total darkness that follows. The first act opens with a scream produced by supernatural possession, the last scene closes with a cry of despair.' While Miss Vallance spoke, her hands flexed and twisted as though she was struggling to free them from the grip of manacles. 'Since we started rehearsals I have put on this mask every night and kept it on till the following morning.

'Not a comfortable way to sleep, but this part must be perfect, Miriam. If I fail a second time – if the countess turns out to be another Saint Joan, I may as well shut up shop.' She spoke very slowly and her face turned towards the tallboy.

'That is the reason for the bandage and I have no intention of removing it because of your absurd suspicions which I hope

– hope – hope that I have now satisfied.' Her voice became louder and she started to stammer.

'Yes, I hope – hope that I have satisfied you, my lords. That you believe in my repentance.' The stammer stopped and her tone became pleading and persuasive. 'I confess to every abomination you have accused me of, but I still crave your indulgence, because I was not a free agent. The Creator of Darkness entered my soul, and I became a tool in his hand.' Miss Vallance was clearly quoting from the script again and far more effectively than she had done at the party.

'Would you condemn a horse because his rider spurs him into battle against you? Is a slave to be blamed for carrying out his master's orders? I was enslaved by the force which I have now renounced and I could not resist his commands. I had to follow him as a river follows its course to the sea.' She bowed to the lifeless pieces of furniture.

'Though I am not asking for your pardon, my lords. I have sinned horribly and no punishment is too severe for my crimes. But for the love of God, whom I mocked and betrayed, grant me one small favour. Do not keep me in darkness any longer. Remove this mask and look at the humility in my face.'

Miss Vallance's spine straightened and she stood in silence waiting for the reply. She was quite oblivious of Miriam and Harry, and the emotion flowing from her body was so intense that they both felt as if they were witnessing the actual scene. The disordered room became the hall of a castle, men at arms were stationed along the walls, and torches lit up the faces of the judges. From the tallboy a voice refused her request and started to pronounce the verdict.

'No – no – no.' The words of disbelief came gasping from Dame Susan's throat and they were followed by a scream which almost made Miriam cry out in unison. The woman's mouth was wide open, her teeth were bared like an animal's, and scream was no way to describe the sound she made. It was a snarl and a whine rising to an agonized howl of hatred and terror, and when it stopped foam dribbled from her chin. Miriam was glad of the bandage at that moment. She was quite sure that the eyes behind it would be as red and glaring as the cloth that screened them.

'She was lying, Miriam.' Harry had leaned across the car and opened the passenger door for her. 'Susan Vallance may be a meticulous actress, but that wasn't the performance of a normal human being. The woman was hepped-up.'

'I agree, but not with drugs.' The scream still rang in Miriam's ears as she climbed in beside him. 'A hallucinogenic drug could have produced the phenomena we witnessed – it could have made Susan believe that she actually was the character she played, but its effects would last for some time. An hour or two at least, and she was her normal, overbearing self when we arrived and the same when we left.'

Miriam considered what had happened when the scream ended. Miss Vallance's hands unclasping and her body sinking into one of the chairs. Emotion had drained her and she looked much older than her forty-odd years.

'I am sorry about that exhibition, Miriam,' she had said after a moment. 'The part is very difficult – very taxing and I have to live with it. I have to get the character just right.' She had wiped her chin with a handkerchief. 'You now know why I wear a blindfold, and I must ask you to excuse me because I really do want an early night.'

'What is that, Mr Clay?' Harry had questioned her and she stood up abruptly. 'Will you please explain yourself?'

'I see.' She listened for a few seconds and then interrupted him with an angry gesture. 'This is quite abominable. First Dr Stanford accuses Paul Trenton of operating on my face, now you have the effrontery to suggest he has been supplying me with drugs.' She hurried to a bell-push. 'You will both leave this flat immediately or I shall get the porters to throw you out.' The door opened, the second maid appeared and led Harry and Miriam away.

'It would be better for Susan if drugs were responsible for her condition.' Miriam spoke uncertainly. 'Drug addicts can often be cured, but a bad case of . . .'

'Of what?' She had fallen silent and Harry prompted her. 'There must be a reason for that frenzy . . . the complete conviction that she was the countess.'

'There is a possible reason, Harry. Susan Vallance could suffer from psychopathic schizophrenia which is virtually incurable, and she may soon be in a very bad way.' While Miriam spoke she thought of another woman's frenzy. Naureen Carlin struggling on the hospital bed before morphine silenced her.

'When Susan first consulted me I felt she was suffering from a mild form of schizophrenia, but I wasn't too worried because the condition is quite common in the theatrical profession, though it usually occurs during a long run. When an actor has played one character for a considerable period he sometimes tends to live the part in real life. Not a serious malady and it soon wears off after the play's run has ended.'

'But that doesn't apply in her case.' Harry was staring through the windscreen. If Miss Vallance had telephoned Doc Trenton and told him about their accusations, the Doc might return to the flat for a face-to-face conference. '*Our Lady of Pain* hasn't even opened.'

'And it may not remain open for more than a week unless Susan can be helped professionally. Intense emotion maintained over a long period is as great a killer as cholera or the plague. It deprives the body of *heparin*, which is needed to clear the arteries of fatty tissues; they fur up and the heart stops.'

'Just as Marty Starr's heart stopped.' Harry was still watching the car-park entrance in the hope that a well-dressed figure carrying a medical bag might appear. 'You said that Miss Vallance once suffered from a fairly harmless form of schizophrenia, Miriam, but you do not consider that drugs are responsible for what we witnessed just now. Could something else have accelerated and multiplied her former condition – maybe hypnosis?'

'I suppose that's possible, provided the hypnotist was extremely talented and extremely wicked.' The memory of Miss Vallance's scream faded and Miriam recalled the photographs Harry had shown her. 'Yes, Trenton could have used hypnosis, he's got to be found and don't you think it's time we went to the police?'

'To tell them what?' Harry was determined to solve the mystery himself and he looked her in the face as he prepared to lie. 'The police know that Trenton was associated with Martin Starr, but they have no evidence to suggest he was involved in the burglary. Nor do you have to be on the medical register to practise hypnosis. Dozens of music-hall entertainers do so.

'No, the police wouldn't listen to us, but we'll find Trenton ourselves. And when we do I'll get the truth out of him if it costs me a spell in prison for Grievous Bodily Harm.

'But I've got a question to ask you.' Harry saw that she had accepted what he said and his eyes returned to the entrance of the car park. 'Is there such a thing as group paranoia? Can it become an epidemic?'

'It's a very common phenomenon and paranoia is merely persecution mania – an unreasoned fear that one is being threatened. I suppose the Nazis' attitude to the Jews is a classic example – also the Northern Ireland business.'

'I don't mean large political or religious movements, because they are inspired by elaborate propaganda machinery.' The idea had just occurred to Harry and he spoke uncertainly. 'I was thinking of small gatherings of individuals who suddenly go insane for no apparent reason.'

'The medieval flagellants come into that category, I suppose.' Miriam tried to remember what she had read on the subject. 'After the Black Death, numbers of people started to roam the countryside flogging themselves in imitation of Christ's agony. They appear to have been terrified of divine punishment and thought that suffering in this world might absolve them.'

'That's the kind of thing I meant.' Harry nodded. 'Weren't there also groups known as the *Choremaniae* – the Mad Dancers? Women who suddenly developed intense sexual cravings but believed they had become sexually repulsive to men. Because of this they tore off their clothes and danced frenziedly in the streets till they collapsed and were trampled to death by their companions.

'Two instances of group mania with no rational cause, and there must have been many more throughout history. Individuals suddenly becoming infected by a force which produced excitement, followed by terror. A mental epidemic, one might say, and I wonder if a similar outbreak has started in this day and age, Miriam.' She was looking at him with open scepticism, but he continued.

'Paul Trenton is the link between four people who have been possessed and terrified. Fergus Carlin killed himself because he feared snakes. Starr's fear of rats stopped his heart beating, and Naureen cannot even name the thing that terrifies her. While Miss Vallance . . .' He thought of the actress's explanation before she started to perform the role: 'The last scene closes with a cry of despair.'

'You consider that the play will end in a week, Miriam, but I think you're over-optimistic and the first night will see it out. Susan Vallance not only believes that she is the countess, she knows what happened to the countess.'

'Yes, I understand your implications, Harry, though I can't go along with all of them.' Miriam looked up at the building. The actress had said she wanted an early night and every window was in darkness. 'If Susan's heart does not stop before the final curtain she'll kill herself as soon as it falls, and so would I if I shared her belief.' She shivered and pulled her coat more tightly around her. 'Death would be a welcome friend if one was about to be walled-up alive.'

## Chapter 10

'There is no need to thank me, Mr Munro.' John Forest prided himself on having a versatile mind and he was carrying on a telephone conversation and studying two sheets of typescript and a quarto-sized colour photograph simultaneously.

'I and the staff of the *Daily Globe* are staunch champions

of law and order and we are always delighted to assist the guardians of the law.' The photograph had been placed under an Anglepoise lamp and the reproductions of gold and silver ornaments studded with gem stones sparkled in its beam. 'The data you sent over this morning will be fully displayed in tomorrow's edition, so let us hope that the publicity reaps results. I only wish we could print the picture in colour, but I'm afraid our directors would not stand the cost. Hard, tight-fisted men, Inspector, who think of little but profit.

'Still, someone may recognize Starr's hoard of ill-gotten gains and come forward.' He looked at Harry who was sitting at the other side of his desk. 'Though I understand you told Clay that the hoard may not be quite so ill-gotten and no actual burglary was involved – not in the general meaning of the word.' He listened to the policeman's answer and nodded.

'Quite so, and I fully appreciate that that is your personal opinion and not for publication.' He frowned at one of the typescripts. 'It does seem as if you're correct, however, because Nathan Adler considers that the collection would fetch over a quarter of a million pounds at a reputable auction. An important sum of money, yet none of the pieces have been reported stolen in this country or abroad.

'Very – very intriguing, Inspector. A treasure trove with items dating from the Middle Ages to the Renaissance, which may have been hidden away generations ago. A miser's hoard perhaps, and the hiding place must have been extremely secure. I'll be delighted to know how Starr discovered it. Also whether there's a connection between his death and the death of Fergus Carlin.

'No comment, eh.' Forest frowned petulantly at the reply. 'Come – come, Mr Munro. You know you can trust me not to release anything till you give the word, and we've done you a great service. If young Clay hadn't been on the scene when Marty Starr went berserk that kid would have had a bullet in her skull. Because Clay knew about Starr's fear of rats and because he risked his life to save Mary Seaton, she is alive and well, and you and your brave boys in blue can take the credit.

Clay's a modest chap and he doesn't want any medals for life-saving.' He gave Harry a cynical grin. 'Oh, I understand, Mr Munro. By "no comment" you mean that nothing was found in the Carlins' flat to connect them with the jewellery business and you're still in the dark.

'A pity, but *nil desperandum* is my motto and I'm sure that you'll crack the case with your customary verve before long. In the meanwhile you can count on the *Globe*'s co-operation and we'll give that picture a really prominent spread.

'Goodbye for the present, Inspector, and the very best of luck.' He lowered the phone into its rest and walked across to his office window. The good weather had blown away during the early morning and it was raining heavily. By some trick of light his face was reflected back at him; grey and puffy and pockmarked by the drops of water spattering the glass.

'From that you will have gathered that the police are getting nowhere, Harry, but just where have you got so far?' He shook his head ponderously. 'Like your friend Dr Stanford, I just can't go along with this group mania notion you've dreamed up. Though I like the possibility that three tough villains like the Starr gang might have been driven mad with remorse because of some crime they committed.' Forest turned and went back to his desk. 'But I'm having second thoughts about that now, and as for a woman like Susan Vallance being associated with a burglary . . . Poppycock!' He picked up the second sheet of typescript which was Harry's progress report.

'I did not say she was involved in the actual robbery, John.' Though Harry had no love for Forest he was beginning to agree with him. Sitting with Miriam in the darkness of the car his last theory had appeared a possibility, but in a brightly lit office with the sound of typewriters clicking through the partitions, it seemed untenable. 'What I did say was that there is a link between Miss Vallance and the Starr people and the link is Trenton.'

'Yes, Trenton, Harry; always Trenton.' The editor lowered himself into his chair. 'Your *bête noire*, the chap who got you into your original mess. We know that he's been treating

Susan Vallance, but what makes you so sure that he was in-volved with Starr and the others?'

'Sorry, but I can't tell you that, John.' Harry pictured the cramped, untidy writing on the sketch plan. 'Not till I've got the full story.'

'And you'd better get the story, son, and get it soon.' The fat man nodded towards a tape-recorder. 'For Munro's benefit the record of our chat on the phone yesterday has been "mucked about a bit", as the music hall ballad goes.'

'I'm sure it has.' Harry knew that parts of the tape would have been erased to make it appear that he was not speaking to Forest, but dictating his findings as a personal memory aid. 'You really are a cruel, slave-driving bastard, John.'

'Cruel – yes. Slave-driver and proud of it – yes. Bastard – no.' Forest chuckled. 'My parents were a most respectable couple and I was born in holy wedlock.

'Yes, I'm driving you, Harry, because I want to publish the story as much as you want to write it. I want to know why those hard cases went gaga, and I want to know where that collection of loot came from.' He opened his cigar box and pushed it across the desk with unusual generosity. 'But though I'm a cruel sod, I promised you a week, and till that week is out you can count on my full support.' He waited for Harry to light a cigar. 'From what you have gleaned up to now it seems that your best bet is to say a prayer. Pray that Naureen Car-lin will recover and Dr Stanford can persuade her to spill the beans and tell her everything. Who put them on to the jewel-lery, where it was hidden, who gave the gang drugs.

'Yes, drugs, son, because that's the only feasible explana-tion.' Harry had started to interrupt and he raised his voice. 'Somebody, maybe Trenton or maybe a character we haven't heard about, fed that trio dope. A stimulant which first encour-aged them to tackle a job quite outside their normal field of operations and then its after-effects completely unhinged them.' Forest scowled at Harry's written report and gave another ponderous shake of the head.

'The fact that no trace of barbiturates, amphetamines,

heroin or what you will was found in Starr's or Naureen Carlin's bloodstream doesn't mean a damn thing. Nor is it significant that there was no pink spot in the urine to show they'd been given L.S.D.

'Hell, science is progressing every day and a completely new substance can have been perfected during the last few days. Something that first stimulates the subjects and then causes schizophrenic fear and depression. A drug whose physical presence is rapidly passed out of the system, but the psychological damage is long-lasting – possibly permanent.' He opened a dog-eared address book and thumbed through the pages.

'Such a preparation may have foxed the police and the hospital analyst, but I know a chap who isn't easily foxed and he might be able to help you.' He had found what he wanted and scribbled down an address and a telephone number. 'Mortimer Veidt at the Central Laboratories. Give Veidt a ring now, mention my name, and make an appointment. At least he'll be able to tell you if the kind of thing I have in mind is scientifically feasible.

'Who wants me, Miss Cathcart?' The telephone had rung as Harry reached out for it and Forest took the call. 'Yes, put him through.

'A fellow killed himself in a tube-station bog, Peter? Which tube-station? Newbury Circus.' He scowled impatiently. 'That's not news, you bloody young fool. They're always croaking down there and "good riddance to bad rubbish" is the only comment I can make. So why the hell are you wasting my time?

'Oh, this one is different is he?' His impatience vanished and he lifted a pencil. 'Naturally I remember that suicide in the church, so tell me more.'

'Yes – yes – yes, I've got that.' He was noting the caller's message on a pad and Harry's thoughts turned to Miriam at the hospital. Was she also taking notes while she listened to a voice, he wondered. To the voice of Naureen Carlin rambling on about the horrors that were torturing her. Or was it possible that Naureen was not rambling, but talking sanely, and

John Forest's hopes were justified? Could she have regained her sanity and be giving Miriam the answers they needed?

'Interesting, Peter, and you can stay with the story.' Forest lowered his pencil. 'Don't budge from the police station till they release the man's name and then call me back immediately.' He replaced the instrument and leaned back in his chair.

'Things may be on the move, Harry. Have you ever visited the Newbury Circus public lavatory in the small hours of the morning?'

'Only once, when I did those articles on teenage vagrancy, and it wasn't a visit I enjoyed.' Harry could remember the experience vividly. Between midnight and 1 a.m. the state-registered heroin addicts received their legal fixes from an all-night chemist near the underground station. After being supplied with disposable syringes and enough heroin to lull their misery for a few hours the majority of the pitiful army staggered down to the lavatory in search of privacy. Some were incontinent, some retched and vomited, all were ill. Many – a great many had hands that shook so badly that the needles slashed their flesh like razors before finding a vein and giving them relief. By the time they left, the cubicles were liberally spattered with blood and the attendants earned every penny of their bonus rates of pay – 'dirty money', as it was called.

'Then you'll understand why I bawled at Peter Lambert when he first gave me the news, Harry. An odd stiff in those bogs is nothing to write home about, but this one is different.' Forest read through his shorthand notes. 'Though an overdose of drugs killed him, the drug was not heroin but barbiturate sleeping-pills. Nor was he a hippy or a teenage drop-out. The fellow was an elderly man with white hair and perfectly respectable, if clothes are anything to go on.' The editor was enjoying keeping Harry in suspense and he paused and took a cigar from the box. 'The two attendants on duty opened the cubicle when they heard him screaming and one of them has a good memory and noted some of his words.' Forest quoted. ' "Fool – damn fool. Forgot the danger . . . Couldn't see to work properly . . . took 'em off." Those were a few of the things he said, but not the important ones.' He snipped the end of his cigar and lit it with agonizing slowness.

'The police haven't released the man's name yet. They've identified him, but want to find if he had any relatives and inform them first. But this is the important thing. Shortly before the joker died he begged the attendants to help him – to protect him from some fiendish supernatural being that had risen from the grave to haunt him.' Forest sucked greedily at the cigar and watched the grey smoke drift across the office. 'The fiendish being had a name, Harry. The fellow thought he was being hounded by the ghost of someone he'd injured . . . someone called Fergus Carlin.'

## Chapter 11

'I agree that the woman is in a bad way, Dr Stanford, but what you suggest might worsen her condition.' Brian Plunket, the dean of the hospital, was an elderly, conservative Irishman with a bristling grey beard that had earned him the nickname of 'Badger' to generations of medical students. 'Two sessions of narco-analysis and one E.C.T. shock have revealed nothing and she has been under almost continuous sedation for a great many hours. No wonder she is weak, with morphine sapping her resistance.'

'Frenzy would have weakened her more, Mr Dean.' Miriam and Plunket were standing beside Naureen Carlin's bed. The woman's face was screened by an oxygen tent and a tube was attached to a vein in her left arm. Through the tube minute quantities of Warfarin were entering the vascular system to prevent the fatty tissues choking the arteries. Warfarin was a safe and effective substance, originally developed as a pesticide which killed vermin by thinning their blood cells and producing internal haemorrhages. But it was not proving effective in this instance. Though still sedated, Naureen's tension was depriving her of heparin, the blood was becoming thicker and thicker and soon it could no longer nourish the heart muscles.

'In my opinion the only chance of saving Miss Carlin is to discover the cause of her disturbance, sir. With that information, I might . . . just might be able to persuade her that her fears are unjustified.'

'Again I agree.' Plunket spoke reluctantly because he disapproved of psychiatrists on principle. 'She is very weak, probably too weak to respond to chemical stimulus.' He reached for her right wrist. The pulse was very fast, but faint and erratic and he could imagine the heart struggling to force blood through the thickening arteries. 'When will her last dose of sedatives start to wear off, Nurse?

'Between five and ten minutes, eh.' He considered the situation. In his opinion, Miriam's proposition was radical and extremely dangerous and might easily overtax the patient, but without help Naureen Carlin would probably die in any case, and he made up his mind.

'Very well, Doctor. I will not interfere and the responsibility is yours, though what you intend to do is most unorthodox. More the methods of the Gestapo than a medical practitioner.'

'Not the Gestapo, Dr Plunket. Pentothal was first used by the Russian secret police.' Miriam shared his repugnance towards the drug in question, but she knew it was the only hope. Naureen Carlin was dying, and even if she could be persuaded to talk and describe her fears, she was probably too far gone to be helped. But the important thing was to make her talk and conventional narcoanalysis had failed. Sodium Pentothal was the last card she had left and also her strongest. 'The patient will be regaining consciousness soon, Mr Dean, and it might be better if Nurse Mackenzie and I were left alone with her.'

'As you wish.' The Badger moved to the door and then turned and looked back. 'The best of luck, Dr Stanford, and luck is a commodity you need. If she dies during this treatment your conscience may trouble you for a long time.' He walked out and closed the door behind him.

'Into whatever house I enter it shall be for the benefit of the sick.' Miriam pondered the Hippocratic oath while she opened her medical bag. Plunket's meaning had been clear

enough. He considered that Miss Carlin should be allowed to
die peacefully under sedation, and if the end came while her
mind was clear and stimulated by Pentothal it would be an
agonizing death full of terror and torment. He might be right,
Miriam thought, but she was not certain. The adrenal activity
suggested that though the woman was asleep and her limbs
relaxed, the unconscious mind still tortured her.

In any event, the risk had to be taken. Harry had telephoned
to give the news that another person might be involved in the
affair. A man who'd killed himself, in the belief that he was
haunted by the ghost of Fergus Carlin. Miriam had scoffed at
Harry's suggestion that a mental epidemic was breaking out,
but now she wasn't sure. If such a thing was even remotely
possible its source had to be located.

'She's coming out of the coma, Doctor.' The nurse had removed the oxygen mask. 'One of the eyelids flickered just now.'

'Good.' Miriam took a hypodermic syringe and two plastic
vials from her bag. One contained strychnine to stimulate the
heart and the other a preparation to loosen the tongue and
make the subject eager to obey a questioner. Sodium Pentothal
– the Soviet Truth Drug which had obtained more confessions
than the rack.

'For the benefit – for the benefit of the sick.' Once again
Miriam recalled the oath. Plunket was correct in saying that
the treatment was reminiscent of the Gestapo and she felt a
twinge of self-disgust while she filled the syringe from each of
the vials and crossed to the bed.

'Thank you.' The nurse had swabbed the patient's free arm
with surgical spirit and she stood aside as Miriam lifted the
wrist. Naureen Carlin's pulse was much more erratic than
when she had last taken it and the sweat glands were ceasing
to function. The skin felt bone dry between her fingers as the
needle pierced a vein and she pressed home the plunger.

Roughly six minutes. That was the time it should take for
the injection to act, if it acted at all. The heart might be too
exhausted to respond to strychnine and some individuals were
resistant to Pentothal.

Five minutes – four minutes. The patient's eyelids fluttered occasionally, but there was no change in the pulse rate and her face was as white as marble.

Three minutes. Miriam glanced at her watch. Its second-hand seemed to be moving with unusual slowness, but the strychnine was beginning to work. The heart beats were more powerful and there was a faint flush on Naureen Carlin's cheeks.

Two minutes. She was coming out of the coma and her eyes were opening. But there was no comprehension in the eyes and her features were as rigid as a death mask.

One minute – Miriam craned over the bed. 'Can you hear me, Naureen?' There was no response and she bent still lower till her mouth was almost touching the patient's ear.

'Listen to me, Naureen. I am a friend and I have come to help you. The only friend who has the power to help you, but in return you must help me. You have to trust me completely and if you do your fears will vanish and you will be safe.' She was getting a reaction now. The eyeballs were wide and staring and the lips were moving, though no sound came from them.

'Tell me everything, Naureen. Tell me when your fears started and what you did to deserve them.' Miriam spoke gently as though she was soothing a child. 'Where did you find that jewellery, Naureen, and who persuaded you and your brother and Starr to steal it?'

'Brother – Fergus. Starr – Marty.' The names were repeated automatically. 'Fergus – good old Fergus.'

'You are not listening, Naureen.' Miriam's tone became sharper. 'I want to know everything, so concentrate hard. What did the three of you do? What happened during that robbery?'

'There wasn't a robbery. We were told we could have what we wanted.' The voice was becoming stronger and so was the pulse. It was becoming too strong. The drugs were overstraining the heart, as Plunket had anticipated, and there might not be much time left. 'Fergus tried to stop me, but I wanted them so badly. "Rings on her fingers – bells on her toes."'

'What did Fergus try to stop you doing, Naureen?' The

woman had started to ramble a nursery rhyme and Miriam forced herself to throw scruples aside. 'Tell me everything that happened or I'll send you to Room One Hundred and One.'

'No – no – no.' The cry was a tiny echo of Miss Vallance's. 'I'm trying to remember, but it's hard – so very hard, and I'm frightened.

'House – house. Yes, we went to a house.' She frowned in concentration. 'Big, cold house. Old, sad, dead house. The place of the child.'

'Where was this house, my dear?' She was obviously trying to relive the experience and Miriam spoke gently again. 'Tell me where the house is and why did you call it by that name? The place of the child.'

'Not name. Can't remember any name, but there were feathers. Feathers and a sheep and a bull. And tar – tar – tar.'

'Feathers and tar.' The first and last words had come gasping out and they suggested a solution to Miriam. 'If that's your fear you can stop worrying, Naureen. You have my promise that nobody is going to tar and feather you.'

'You fool.' Miriam's guess had been wrong but it had one desired effect and the woman's anger made her almost lucid. 'You think that's all they want to do to me, and you don't understand a bloody thing. You haven't a clue what I did and how I must pay for it.' The heart beats were pounding now and she tried to pull her arm away from Miriam. 'Pay – pay for my sin. Mine and Fergus's and Marty Starr's.

' "Rings on her fingers and bells on her toes." ' Clarity faded and the rhyme rambled from her lips once more. ' "She shall have music wherever she goes." Lovely bells – beautiful shiny bells. Bells and rings and bangles. I wanted them – wanted them so badly and I took out my knife and . . .' The sentence was interrupted by a harsh rattle, the heart gave a final thud and stopped.

There was no hope of reviving her with artificial respiration and Miriam released the lifeless wrist. She knew that the nurse would be looking at her with either pity or disapproval and either emotion was justified. Her experiment had accelerated the patient's death and the information she had gained seemed unimportant. Naureen Carlin had died in anguish, as her brother and her partner had died. As an unknown man in a public lavatory had died.

A worthless and cruel attempt to discover the truth, or was it? Miriam stood up thoughtfully. Naureen Carlin had not been able to name the house where the crime took place, but had she suggested what kind of house it was? Feathers and tar – a sheep and a bull . . . Perhaps a farmhouse.

# Chapter 12

'Even allowing for its amateurish execution this was not intended to depict a common-or-garden farmhouse, Mr . . . er . . . Clay.' Professor Brigham-Beer, curator of the National Heritage Museum, had allowed Harry a further ten minutes of his valuable time. 'All the same, crippling taxation has driven many of our landed gentry into gainful employment and farming is a popular occupation.' He laid aside Starr's plan and leaned back in his chair.

'You say that some notes you found amongst Edgar Mayne's manuscript material suggested that he intended to carry out a psychical investigation at this place and there was a mention of animals; sheep and cattle?'

'Also tar and feathers, Professor Beer.' John Forest's drug expert at the Central Laboratories was out of England and Harry had taken a taxi to the museum after Miriam had telephoned and described Naureen Carlin's death. The route passed near Newbury Circus and he had stopped at the police station and spoken to Peter Lambert, the reporter covering the suicide case. The dead man's name was still being kept a secret, but a talkative desk sergeant had told Lambert that he was definitely not a drop-out. In the pockets of his well-pressed suit was a wallet containing thirty-three pounds, a silver cigarette-case, a pair of spectacles and a pair of polaroid sun-glasses with amber-tinted lenses. Also the bottle which had once held the pills that killed him.

'Feathers and tar, Mr Clay. You are beginning to interest me, because for some reason the connection rings a bell in my mind.' The professor closed his eyes and concentrated for a moment. 'The trouble is that I have accumulated such a vast store of knowledge over the years that my brain is like an over-worked telephone exchange, and occasionally it is difficult to select the right number.

'Perhaps some liquid refreshment might help.' He leaned forward, opened a desk drawer and produced a bottle and a brandy balloon. 'Yes, this should stimulate the grey matter, so have no fear. The number will be found and the connection made in time.'

'My guess is that the house might be a farm surrounded by pine woods.' Harry would have liked a drink himself, but it was quite clear that his host had no intention of offering him one. 'Or near a factory or timber yard where tar is extracted, Professor Beer.'

'Your guesses are supremely unimportant, Mr Clay, so do not interrupt my thought process.' The curator poured him-self a stiff measure of brandy and sniffed at it before drinking. 'Also let me remind you that my name is Brigham-Beer. There are many Beers in the world, but I am Sir Hector Brigham-Beer.' He lowered the glass, recorked the bottle, and propped his jowl on his right fist in the attitude of Rodin's "Thinker".

'To tar and feather a person. An unpleasant practice usually inflicted on vagrants and loose women. Once common in the United States of America and prevalent in Ireland today. I have always believed that wogs begin at Dublin as well as Calais.' He cackled at his witticism. 'But the pastime has never been widespread in this country, so I wonder if an isolated instance once occurred and a nickname came into being.

'You know the kind of thing – often happens with pubs. There's one in North Wales with the outlandish name of The Brondanwy Arms but it's always referred to as The Ring. An enterprising landlord used to organize boxing matches in the back yard.' Brigham-Beer's study was shelved from floor to ceiling and he took another swig of brandy and pointed at a case on his right. 'The *Dictionary of Rural Topography* might help, so go and fetch me Volume Two, Clay.

'Don't dither about, man.' Harry had found what he wanted and was holding out a heavy tome, but the professor was too lordly a person to lift a finger for himself. 'Put it down on the desk.

'Now, let me see.' He opened the book and frowned. 'A hotel in Devon is known as Tarry Jack's Kitchen because sailors used to stop there on their way to Plymouth. Lethbridge Grange is called Tiny Tim's place – one of the owners was a dwarf.' He thumbed busily through the pages while he spoke.

'Ah, what's this? Tarbrush Manor, that's pretty close.' He read the entry and grunted. 'Umhm, another bloody dud. The place was pulled down years ago and the name arose because the family had darker complexions than our northern sun usually produces; pepper-and-salt jobs presumably.

'No, there's no association with tarring and feathering, I'm afraid.' The phone rang as Brigham-Beer closed the book and he lifted the receiver.

'The Creator here.' Harry stifled a gasp. The man must have intended to say *curator*, but it definitely sounded as though he had announced himself as the maker of the universe. 'I am quite aware that the ten minutes I promised Mr Clay have expired, Miss Hedges, but I have decided to extend them.

'Who did you say is calling? Oh, only Lord Swineham. Common little socialist pen-pusher elevated to the peerage by the Wilson administration.' He pulled out a gold half-hunter watch and glowered at the dial. 'Tell him to ring me back after luncheon.

'No, on second thoughts, you can scrub that, Miss Hedges. I don't want to talk to the blighter, so tell him not to bother to call me. Say I'm intensely busy and will contact him at my earliest convenience.' He slammed down the phone and grinned at Harry. 'Which means never, Clay. Swineham's trying to persuade the Department of the Environment to purchase

Danemere Castle and turn it into a rest home for retired In-
land Revenue officials. Wants me to admit that the place is of
no historical or architectural interest.' The professor emptied
his brandy glass and uncorked the bottle for another helping.

'The little toad's right of course. Danemere Castle is just a
mouldering Victorian barn and completely uninteresting. The
only dramatic event that happened there was the death of a
third earl. He used to smoke cigars in bed when he was tight,
set fire to a feather mattress and went up in his own smoke.'
Brigham-Beer raised the bottle. 'All the same, I intend to fight
Swineham to the last ditch. Rest home for tax-gatherers –
Pahr!'

'What's the matter, Professor?' At first Harry had imagined
that his sudden dark flush had been caused by irritation at
Lord Swineham's scheme, but there was more to it than that.
He had closed his eyes again and he continued to pour out
the brandy though its amber liquid was overflowing across the
desk and on to his trousers. Harry reached out and took the
bottle from him. 'Are you ill?'

'I am perfectly well, Clay, and I am also bloody angry.' The
professor opened his eyes and if looks could kill Harry would
have dropped dead in his chair. 'On two occasions you have
come here and wasted my time with demands for information, because your miserable newspaper wants to do an article
on Edgar Mayne, the ghost hunter.' He glowered at the plan
which lay soaking in alcohol. 'If you hadn't misled me with
inaccurate data I could have solved the problem immediately.'
He stood up and Harry saw that his ill-temper was on the
mend.

'An absorbing topic, however, and strangely enough one
of my assistants told me that somebody else made a similar
inquiry when I was on vacation last June.' He stomped over to
a card index file. 'While I find the references you can clear up
that damn mess, Clay.'

'With pleasure, Sir Hector.' Harry pulled out his handkerchief and started to swab the desk. Enlightenment was in sight
and he'd have cleaned Brigham-Beer's boots if the professor

had asked him to. 'You know which house Edgar Mayne was interested in?'

'Yes, and you either read his notes incorrectly or Mayne was senile and wrote in riddles. Probably the latter, because he was pushing ninety when he died.' He selected a card, read it through quickly and moved to a bookcase. 'You got the words all wrong, Clay, and if that blasted Swineham hadn't phoned I might have wasted hours following false trails. Recalling the Earl of Danemere's fiery death in a feather bed put an end to the confusion you created in my mind, however, and Bob is a close relative.' The professor returned to the desk with a small quarto volume and waited for Harry to finish his charring operations.

'The house is near Delford in Essex and it was built by a family named Holtby during the reign of Queen Elizabeth the First.' The desk was fairly respectable once more and he sat down. 'The place has never been a farm and the mention of sheep and cattle can be explained by the Holtby coat-of-arms. *Un bélier rampant et un taureau couchant.*

'That means a male sheep standing up and a bull lying down.' Harry's face had remained blank and Brigham-Beer translated scornfully. 'You really are an ignorant young man. I used the French form because "Ram rampant" sounds bloody silly.

'The house is named Flethertarn Hall, which suggests that the Holtbys were of north-country origin and called their new home after some stretch of water in Cumberland or Westmorland. I presume you know that tarn is the general term for a lake or a large pond in those counties.' He opened the book at a woodcut which showed a rambling cluster of buildings with the sea behind them. 'The Holtbys are now extinct and the land has been bought by a property company who intend to develop the site. So I'd advise you to get cracking with your ghost hunt as soon as possible.'

'Ghost hunt?' Harry leaned over his shoulder to look at the print. 'It is definite that the place is supposed to be haunted?'

'Definite is not a word one can apply to the supernatural,

Clay, and I would have thought that even a journalist would know that.

'But old Mayne must have considered the possibility of a ghost, and Dr Cyrus Tweed, the author of this book, was an extremely eminent Victorian scholar. If Tweed is right, the demolition workers may be in for quite a shock when they pull the building down.' The professor chuckled maliciously over the text.

'In Tweed's view, the Holtby legend was based on fact and something rather objectionable happened at Flethertarn Hall.' He paused for emphasis and repeated almost the exact words Harry had last heard through the partition of the Feathers public house. 'Something nasty – very nasty indeed.'

' "The whereabouts of the room was only known to the head of the family and the bailiff till the male heir reached his seventh birthday." ' Brigham-Beer read from Tweed's book. ' "The child was then given the information, but made to swear that he would never profit from his knowledge. This tradition was discontinued by Sir Gilbert Holtby in 1828, however, and the hiding-place is now a complete secret.

' "Some years ago, the late Mrs Isabel Holtby visited the deathbed of a bailiff named Playfair, who had served the family all his life, and asked him what the room contained. To this the old man replied as follows. 'Mrs Holtby, I do not know what is inside that room, but I believe we should both thank God that we do not know. For if you did know the secret of your house you would be a most unhappy woman.' " ' The professor guffawed.

'I bet the poor girl had a sleepless night after that answer, Clay.' His good humour had returned and though he claimed to be a busy man he seemed to have plenty of time to spare. 'A fascinating yarn, and there must be some foundation to it. The ritual was stopped after an estate mason committed suicide and Sir Gilbert Holtby seemed to think he was personally responsible for the man's death.

'Nothing to that, perhaps, but I seem to remember that

there was another suicide not so long ago.' He laid down the book and adopted his Rodin pose. 'Yes, the last owner of the house was not a Holtby, but a chap called Carslake, and he went round the bend. They put him in a state asylum and he either hanged himself or slit his throat with a pair of scissors he'd stolen from one of the nurses. Can't recall which method he used, but it was one or the other and they're both unpleasant ways to go.'

'Horrible ways.' Harry thought of Fergus Carlin's throat and once again he asked himself if the man would be alive without his intervention. 'I gather that there's no definite evidence as to what's hidden in the house, Professor.'

'Definite! How you love that word, Clay.' Brigham-Beer snorted. 'No, there's nothing one could call evidence, but a great deal of supposition. Dr Tweed, who wrote this book at the end of the last century, wouldn't venture a definite opinion, though I've got a hunch that there must have been a case of teratology; a monstrous birth and . . .' The telephone was ringing again and he scowled. 'Drat that blasted contraption. Can I never have any peace?

'Miss Hedges, I'm engaged in an important piece of historical research and must not be disturbed.

'Who – what?' Brigham-Beer had been irritated when he lifted the receiver, but his manner changed abruptly. His leathery face paled, his body seemed to shrink inside his suit, his free hand trembled. 'Christ – I forgot – it completely slipped my mind.' He stared helplessly at his watch. 'You say that she's on the line now, Miss Hedges?

'Then please apologize most profusely and tell her that I was unavoidably detained and will be along directly. Say that it's your fault and you forgot to remind me of the appointment.' He cupped a hand over the mouthpiece while the message was delivered.

'My wife, Clay. Supposed to have met her in a restaurant twenty minutes ago. Impatient woman – spirited temper – very angry. I'll have to dash, but you can borrow Tweed's book, and I'll be interested to read your article.

'Well, Miss Hedges, did Lady Brigham-Beer accept that you are to blame for the delay? That you should have reminded me?' A slight touch of his usual pomposity returned, but only briefly and he became even more abject. 'All right, put her through.

'Is that you Penelope? Darling, I can't say how dreadfully sorry I am. All my secretary's fault – let me get caught up with a wretched journalist fellow – most irresponsible girl – shockin' business.' He cringed and grovelled, but it got him nowhere. An indignant female voice rasped from the earpiece and Harry heard the words, 'Liar – coward – poltroon.' Though he hadn't liked 'wretched journalist fellow,' he sympathized with the professor's humiliation and saw the cause of it glowering from a photograph on the mantelshelf. Lady Brigham-Beer was a hulking cruiser of a woman with a face designed to awe children, servants and social inferiors. She probably numbered 99.9 per cent of the human race in the last category and the picture showed her dressed for the hunting field. Booted and spurred and looking as if she would enjoy plying the riding whip that dangled from her hand.

'Sitting alone in a third-rate restaurant for almost half an hour, Hector. No manners – no consideration – no concern for others. Self – self – self is your only motto . . .' The recriminations poured out, punctuated by feeble excuses from the recipient, and ended with 'I shall wait exactly fifteen minutes, Hector, and not a second longer.'

'What are you hanging about for Clay?' The phone had gone dead and Brigham-Beer shot from his chair like a bolted rabbit. 'I said you can borrow the book, so be off with you.

'Christ almighty!' He had noticed a damp patch on his trousers. 'Brandy! I must reek of the stuff and Penelope can't stand the smell. Makes her feel sick – gives her headaches and hot flushes.'

'I'm sure the smell will have worn off by the time you get to the restaurant.' Harry slipped the book into his briefcase. 'You've been extremely kind, Professor, but there's just one more thing that might help me. Can you recall the name of the other man who inquired about the house?'

'Don't think so. I told you I was away when the person called.' Brigham-Beer was adjusting his tie very carefully. 'Seem to remember my assistant saying it was a name like Nally or Rally. Something of that kind, but what the hell does it matter?' He put on a Homburg hat and hurried off to his delayed appointment and a most disagreeable meal.

# Chapter 13

A name like Nally or Rally. Did that mean the other inquiry had been an innocent one, quite unconnected with the robbery, or was a fourth person involved? Perhaps the white-haired man who had killed himself in the tube-station. Harry had hired a taxi to take him to Essex and the borrowed book was open on his knees. *An Account of the Mythology and Folk Beliefs of East Anglia*, by the Rt Rev. Cyrus Tweed, D.D. A pompous title and a pompous author whose literary style bore a strong resemblance to Brigham-Beer's manner of speech. When Brigham-Beer wasn't speaking to his wife, of course.

Nally or Rally – something of the kind. Harry had hoped that the professor might have said Starr or Carlin or Trenton, but maybe one of the gang had used a pseudonym. Not very likely, because credentials were needed to penetrate the inner sanctums of the National Heritage Museum. Both a porter and a secretary had checked his press card before letting him through into the curator's domain. If the inquiry had been connected with the robbery, the caller might have been the recent suicide.

But, as Brigham-Beer had said, what the hell did a name matter, and the police would be bound to release the dead man's identity soon. Harry tried to ignore the rattle of the cab's diesel engine and a screeching transistor radio on which the driver was listening to a football match. The important thing was that he was on his way to the right place. The sketch Trenton had given Starr might not be drawn to scale but the book contained an interior plan of Flethertarn Hall and the drawings obviously corresponded. Harry's drug theory was on the wane and he had become more and more certain that something which occurred during the raid was responsible for the group mania. Providing the house had not been demolished already he might discover the truth in the immediate future.

'The Delford region of Essex was notorious for witch hunts during the early seventeenth century, and when Sir Arthur Holtby returned from France with a foreign bride, suspicious eyes were turned in his direction.' Harry had skipped quickly through the chapter dealing with the Flethertarn affair and he started to reread the pertinent passages. 'These suspicions were not unnatural, for in his youth Sir Arthur was said to have led a most profligate life. Though he claimed to have repented, many people doubted this and a wave of sickness in the area was attributed to his homecoming. His wife, whose name I have suppressed because she came from a family who are still well regarded in Europe, is believed to have been a mocker of God and human dignity. It certainly seems likely that she was a cruel and vicious woman who soon aroused the hostility of her neighbours.'

*Was said – is believed to have been – certainly seems likely*, Harry frowned at the text. Brigham-Beer had told him that the Rt Rev. Cyrus Tweed was an eminent scholar, but the work contained no reference index, no bibliography, and appeared to be largely based on hearsay and the author's imagination.

'Probably the woman's death during childbirth caused much local rejoicing and tradition suggests that her sins were visited on her child; a monstrously deformed creature, so hideous that only the father could bear to look upon her.'

'A wonderful save by Swan and it's a corner for Clapham United.' Applause and a commentator's voice roared from the radio to interrupt Harry's reading. 'Jack Clark's taking the kick, Tynecastle are packing the goal mouth and . . . Ahhrr . . .' There was a dismal wail. 'What a poor header by Wiggy Bennet. Right over the net.'

'That bloody Bennet couldn't nod a ball through the Admiralty Arch.' The taxi-driver turned and spoke through the partition window. 'Christ knows why they picked him. Still it's a fast, open game and a nice day for it.'

'Good job the rain's blown over.' Harry grunted in agreement. They had left the dual carriageway and were on a minor road skirting the Essex marshes. The sea was shimmering in the sunlight and a big oil-tanker was clawing its way towards the Thames estuary. She lay so low in the water that her catwalks were awash and the stern and midships superstructures looked as though they belonged to two separate vessels.

'All I know is that the house is somewhere near Delford.' Harry replied to the driver's question. 'We'd better go into the village and ask.'

'This unfortunate child vanished in her early youth and was never heard of again.' Harry read on. 'One tradition states that she was claimed by the mysterious malady that had followed Sir Arthur's return, another that she was stolen by gypsies who considered she possessed magical powers, a third that she was murdered by her father and secretly buried.

'The last version is unlikely, because Sir Arthur was clearly grief-stricken by her loss and a rumour became current that to avoid the reminders of his wife and child he hid the former's jewellery in a sealed cache.' Harry nodded, recalling the collection in Starr's flat. At least one of Tweed's suppositions appeared to be true.

'A year after his daughter's disappearance, Arthur Holtby remarried and the union was blessed with a fine, healthy son. On his seventh birthday this boy was made to swear an oath of silence and then told the location of a secret room that had been built into the fabric of the house. He was also instructed to confide this knowledge to his own heir when he reached the same age. The Holtby tradition had started and it was to continue for almost two hundred years.' Harry turned a page. 'There is no knowing what the room contained, or still contains, and idle conjecture is valueless.' Tweed's style really was reminiscent of Brigham-Beer. 'However, while Sir Gilbert Holtby was on his deathbed, he hinted that he had concealed vast riches somewhere in the house, but they were well guarded and anyone rash enough to steal them would rue the day he was born. These statements were recorded by the Vicar of Delford whose diary was published by the Viceroy Press and a copy is in my possession.'

Good for you, Cyrus Tweed, Harry thought. At last a piece of definite evidence had been offered and he imagined what must have occurred on those seventh birthdays. A small, nervous boy swearing an oath, and then being shown a wall behind which great wealth lay hidden. Was he also told that that treasure had a guardian? Harry's belief that Trenton had given Starr and the others drugs had vanished from his mind. Like Dr Tweed he had few facts at his disposal, but instinct told him that the phenomenon must stem from something which existed long before modern medicine.

Guardian or no guardian, the knowledge must have been a sore temptation to the heirs, because Sir Arthur's cache had been considerable. The medallion in Starr's flat was worth a fortune on its own; the work of Benvenuto Cellini, one of the world's finest craftsmen.

And it appeared that at least two people had yielded to temptation in the past. The ritual had been ended by Gilbert Holtby after a stonemason committed suicide, and the last owner of the house, David Carslake, had killed himself in a lunatic asylum. Had the mason cut through the wall on his master's orders? Had Carslake followed his example?

What of the present-day actors in the drama; Starr and the Carlins? One had died at home, one in a church, one in hospital. Also Mr Anonymous taking his overdose of pills in a public lavatory because he believed Carlin's ghost was pursuing him. The place and manner of their deaths was unimportant, but they had all died because they were frightened and it seemed more and more likely that their fears had originated at Flethertarn Hall.

'I think this is it.' Harry rapped on the partition and raised his voice, because the driver was engrossed in the football match. Beyond the trees and a wall flanking the road he had seen a big house, and a hundred yards farther on was a telephone booth and a pair of tall, wrought-iron gates.

'Stop by the phone-box please.' The cab drew up and Harry climbed out and examined the gates. They were securely locked and two notices were attached to their railings. One stated that the Happy Home Construction Company had received planning permission to build fifty bungalows on the site. The other issued a stern warning to deter squatters, campers, trespassers and other undesirables.

'How much do I owe you?' Harry returned to the taxi. His investigation might take several hours and he could find transport back to London in Delford, which was only a mile or so away. He paid the driver and watched him turn round and move off with the radio blasting the quiet countryside. The cab was out of sight before Harry realized that he had left his briefcase and Brigham-Beer's book on the seat, and he shrugged and entered the phone-box.

The *Globe*'s switchboard answered immediately, but Forest's extension was engaged and Harry's supply of loose change had almost run out when he finally heard the editor's voice. 'Yes, there is news indeed, my boy. News that will surprise you.' Once again Forest was enjoying keeping him in suspense. 'The police have released the name of the Newbury Circus stiff, and I'll bet you a quid that you can't guess who he was. An elderly fellow with white hair. Any ideas?'

'Not a clue, John, and please stop playing games.' Harry had one two-pence piece left. 'I'm in a public call-box and we'll be cut off soon.'

'So what? You can always ring back and get the operator to transfer the charge, and I wish to congratulate you.' A chair creaked as the fat man eased his bulk into a more comfortable position. 'I always thought you were on to a good story, but I never realized just how good. Nor did I believe the notion that intense shock can change the colour of a person's hair. I imagined it was just an old wives' tale, but apparently I've been wrong.' The terminal pips sounded and Harry slipped his last coin into the slot. 'The chap who killed himself in Newbury

Circus tube-station had brown hair before his death, but it was snow-white when the attendant found him.' Forest paused to let the information sink in.

'Yes, Harry, the corpse belonged to your bugbear – Paul Trenton.'

Trenton was dead. He had gone the same way as the Carlins and Martin Starr, which suggested that he had not merely planned the raid and given them the map. Doc Trenton had been an active member of the team and taken part in the robbery.

Harry had climbed the wall and he walked slowly down the winding tree-lined drive leading to the house. Very slowly; his feet dragged over the ruts and pot holes that pitted the route and he had to force himself to keep moving. Something inside Flethertarn Hall must have been responsible for at least four deaths and very soon he might experience its powers himself. All the same, he had come so far that he had to go on, whatever the risk. He had to know the truth or despise himself for the rest of his life.

In the woodcut and viewed from the road the house had looked gloomy and sinister, but when Harry rounded a bend his second sight of it looked pleasant enough. A low U-shaped building with bow windows, Jacobean chimneys and an imposing gothic porch. The afternoon sun glowed on the mellow brickwork and, though the place was clearly deserted, it had an air of welcome and he almost expected that when he reached the porch the door would open and some apple-cheeked housekeeper appear to greet him.

But the welcoming air vanished as he drew closer. The brickwork which had looked mellow in the distance was rotten and crumbling, and had not been repointed for decades. Many of the graceful windows lacked glass and had been boarded up, one of the chimneys had fallen and torn a gaping hole in the roof, a stretch of loose guttering sagged above the porch. The last occupant had been a poor man who died in a public asylum. Perhaps he was poor enough to have defied the curse and searched for Sir Arthur Holtby's treasure.

'Go back, you fool. Back – back – back.' Mingled with a murmur of bees and the cries of birds, a voice in Harry's head started to warn him and he hesitated when he reached the shadow formed by the southern wing of the house. 'You can't solve the problem, Clay, so leave it to the professionals. Go back – get away from here and contact the police.' The voice became louder and more insistent; what it said was true and Harry felt a twinge of relief as he saw that the door had a heavy padlock fitted to the frame. He was mad to have come on his own and he could never search the building single-handed. He had to forget about writing a scoop, make a clean breast of everything to Inspector Munro and take the consequences.

'That's right, Clay. You're coming to your senses aren't you?' The voice was as clear as though its owner was speaking in his ear. 'You know why Marty Starr's heart stopped beating – You know why Fergus Carlin cut his throat and Naureen died raving – You know what turned Trenton's hair white. The treasure had a guardian and that guardian is free. A hole in the wall has released it, so go back – back – back.'

'Don't be a coward, Harry.' Another imaginary voice addressed him, the voice of Miriam Stanford. 'You can't run away now. You have to discover the truth and write your story. We must know what happened in this building, so break open the door and find out.' The second voice was the more persuasive and Harry walked up the steps to the porch and lit a cigarette to steady his nerves. As the match flickered he saw a carved slab set in the brickwork that had been hidden by shadow and he struck another.

HIC EST ECCE PROGENIES FAMILIARIS HOLTBYENSIS. The sentence was cut deep in the stone and lines of dates and proper names lay beneath it. The first date was 1586, the last 1930, and though Harry's Latin was negligible there was no doubt that he was looking at the Holtby family tree preserved since the house was built.

A strange conceit, he thought, and then he recalled the omission that Dr Tweed had deliberately made in his book, and he took another match from the box. When it flared, a name seemed to leap out of the slab like a missile and he turned and walked away from the porch.

But not away from the house. Another piece of information had been provided and he had to obey the voice of Miriam Stanford. He hunted around the grounds till he found a rusty pickaxe and returned to prise off the lock.

# Chapter 14

Flethertarn Hall appeared to be a house of moods. Gloomy when viewed from the road, friendly and welcoming as Harry approached, then more hostile and threatening than any building he had known.

But once he had made up his mind and started work on the door the atmosphere changed again, and though his anxieties remained, Harry's fears vanished. There was nothing hostile about the place, nothing to be frightened of, but neither was there any welcome or friendliness. The house was just an old, decayed building waiting to be torn down, and so lifeless that he imagined it had been unoccupied for several years.

Cold too – deathly cold. The padlock had come away from the frame and the door creaked open and he stepped into a wide, low-ceilinged entrance hall. A staircase faced him with doors at either side of it and open passages led away from the walls on his right and left. The air might have been refrigerated and Harry turned up the collar of his jacket. He had expected the house to be cold, but not that kind of coldness. Judging from the exterior, the place looked as though it would be damp, with mouldering plaster and rotting woodwork, but the opposite was true. The wallpaper was faded and here and there were darker patches to show where pictures and furniture had been positioned, but the plaster was obviously sound and the floorboards had no sag or give in them. One of the windows had a broken pane and sand had blown in from the sea and coated the floor with a fine carpet that crunched beneath his feet. The place was as dry and antiseptic as an operating theatre and mildew and rot had gained no headway. While he looked around and considered how to start his search, Harry noticed that there was not a spider's web to be seen, though a few dead flies lay on the windowsills.

Which way should he go? He cursed himself for leaving the book and Starr's plan in the taxi. The house was shaped like an open rectangle and an illustration in the book had shown that one of the wings had been added to the original structure. Harry was no architect, all the three blocks had appeared similar in date and style to his untrained eyes, and he couldn't remember which was the addition. He decided to take the left-hand corridor first, walked five paces towards it and then stopped dead in his tracks.

He had been wrong. The house might appear lifeless, but it was occupied. He had company and other feet were moving across the floor. Unfriendly feet which must belong to a spy, because they stopped at the same instant he did. Either squatters or tramps were in residence or a watchman was on duty and had noted his presence.

'All right.' He turned and looked around the shadowy hall. 'I know you've seen me, so where are you?'

'All right – all right – all right. I know – know – know . . .' There was no one in sight, but his words had been repeated after a pause, and Harry relaxed. Stripped of furniture and carpeting the place was a trap for echoes and he was quite alone. He walked on down the corridor and then stopped again with a frown. The passage had a rather attractive marble arch and a cornerstone bearing the date 1802. The jewels were much earlier than that and their hiding place must be elsewhere. He returned to the hall and headed for the right-hand corridor. His steps crunched on the sand and echoed from the boards and he tried to imagine how the earlier search had been carried out, and how the gang first learned about the treasure.

Trenton's marginal note on the sketch he'd given Starr stated that the thing was 'a rough plan which our informant drew from memory', and Professor Brigham-Beer described it

as a childish scrawl. The professor had been speaking colloqui-
ally, but the description might be completely accurate, because
Fergus Carlin had implied that a child had been attacked during the robbery. Harry shivered as a solution occurred to him
and not merely because the house was so cold.

Was it possible that a local child playing in the empty house
had found the treasure trove by chance and taken some of
the jewellery? Her parents and friends would never have suspected that her finds were valuable. Solid gold and silver set
with precious stones. They'd have accepted the story that she
had bought some cheap trinkets in a bazaar or junk shop. The
child's secret would have been quite safe till one day she was
seen by someone who knew about jewellery.

'What a lovely bracelet you're wearing, my dear. Who gave
it to you?' The voice would have been friendly and its owner
the sort of person to invite confidences. 'You found it, did you?
How very clever of you. And the rings as well, I suppose.

'There were other things there, too? What a lucky girl you
are! I've got some friends who would love to visit your hidey-
hole, so would you take us to it? Say yes, and I'll buy you more
toys and sweets than you've ever dreamed about.

'Draw a little picture of the place and then we'll all come
and see you soon.'

Yes, that could have been the start of the story, Harry
thought, as he walked on down the corridor, pausing to peer
into empty rooms which showed no sign of having been disturbed. The original finder of the treasure trove could have
led her new friends there, but Carlin's suggestion was that she
had been knifed. That seemed to disprove the theory because
the files showed that no child had been attacked or reported
missing in the area for several months.

What was that? A slow tapping sound was coming from
around a bend in the corridor and he moved forward more
cautiously. Only an open window swinging in the breeze and
banging against the frame, but it brought him to an abrupt
halt. The window had been recently forced, there were inden-
tations in the woodwork where a chisel or a jemmy had been

inserted and the broken catch showed a glint of bright metal. As in the hall, sand had blown through the opening on to the floor, but another substance was mingled with it. White powdery stuff like flour stretching away along the passage.

There was no doubt what the powder was. The thieves had entered by the window and they had cut through a wall. Powdered plaster had stuck to their shoes and marked the return journey.

Harry followed the trail, which was not hard to follow, and now and again he saw evidence that the gang had been unsure of their destination. Footprints in the sand which were free of plaster proved that they had inspected several rooms before moving on down the corridor again.

The trail ended at an open door beyond which there was no trace of plaster or footprints, and the room behind the doorway had a flagstone floor and two windows. The sun was shining through their dusty glass, but the room was even colder than the rest of the house he had visited and as arid as a desert. A big fireplace of bricks and iron faced the windows and one glance told Harry that he had reached his goal. Piles of rubble littered the flagstones and gaps around the fireplace showed that the unit had been torn away from the wall and then moved back. Above it, a ray of sunlight was directed at a dark hole in the chimney breast.

'Are you insane, Clay? Do you want to share the Carlins' agony – to die raving like Starr and Trenton? Don't you realize the forces you're up against?' The first voice repeated its warnings, but Miriam's voice urged him on.

'Don't be afraid, Harry. Take hold of the fireplace and drag it away from the wall.'

Though the room was icy, Harry's body was damp with sweat, but once again he obeyed Miriam's imaginary commands. He planted his feet firmly to gain a purchase, grasped the mantelshelf and braced his back. To move such a mass of brick and metal would be a hard task for one man and a sudden violent jerk was essential. He counted three and pulled. Without any resistance the whole unit pivoted forward and threw him sideways. His skull crashed on the floor and the sunlight vanished.

He could only have been unconscious for a second or two, because when he raised his head the fireplace was still creaking on the rusty hinges which had helped to hold it in position. But it seemed an eternity since he had tugged at the mantelshelf and at first he imagined that he had broken his contact lenses because everything appeared blurred and distant.

His vision cleared after a while, however, and he saw that the fireplace was a dummy. No flue connected it to a chimney, no coal or logs had ever burned in its grate. The thing was a camouflaged door which had been cemented to the wall after its usefulness ended. A solid barrier before the bricks and mortar were chipped away and the bolts withdrawn.

It took Harry some time to realize what the door had screened, though he appeared to be looking into a miniature chapel. A little room with russet-coloured walls inscribed with crosses and stars, pentagons and triangles, and other mystic symbols. There was also a wooden crucifix and a stone font, a table, a chair and a bed.

But several more seconds passed before Harry noticed the occupant of the room and when he stood up and looked at her closely he was violently sick, though there had been nothing horrific about her appearance in life. It was what had been done to her that made him vomit.

A tiny, copper-skinned woman was lying on the couch. She wore a faded red gown, and though her body was thin and wasted, its posture suggested she had died quietly, which was hard to believe. Her two slim, brown hands lay on the floor some distance away from the stumps of her wrists, and she had no eyes. They had been gouged out and an earwig was wriggling in one of the empty sockets.

# Chapter 15

Not a woman, not an Indian, and she had not been tortured or murdered – at least not within the life-span of any ordinary person. Harry stood staring down at the couch. The body belonged to a child who had been dead for over three hundred years and she had died of boredom and misery and neglect. She was the daughter of Sir Arthur Holtby and he had locked her away because her appearance distressed her fellow beings. After she died, the door of the cell had been sealed and the cold, dry atmosphere had halted decay and her flesh became mummified.

The yellow insect was still crawling in the eye socket and Harry looked away. When he was young he had been told that earwigs were so-named because they could enter the ear passage and bore into one's brain. He knew the story was untrue and the creatures were harmless, but he still disliked them intensely.

Not only the cell had created darkness for the girl. Even when the door opened to provide her with food she had been denied light. Harry lifted an object from the floor. A leather visor like the hood of a hawk with slits for the mouth and nose, and a lock to ensure that the wearer could never be free of her mask. The poor wrinkled face was free now, of course. At some period the lock had been released and Harry had a strong suspicion why. Sir Arthur was thought to have hidden away his wife's jewels and he had obviously hidden his daughter with them. After the child died was it possible that perversity had prompted him to remove her eyes and replace them with precious stones?

The legend and what Harry had discovered for himself suggested that that might be true, but two points still baffled him. What had guarded the cell, and why had the child been so mercilessly treated? Dr Tweed's suggestion was that she had been a hideously deformed monstrosity, but Tweed was wrong. Though shrunk and wizened by time, the body showed no trace of deformity and in life the prisoner would have been a physically normal little girl.

So why? Just why had such a living hell been inflicted on her, and what was the meaning of the crucifix and the font, and the symbols on the walls? Most of the signs had been painted on the plaster, but there were one or two actual objects, and Harry reached for a disc hanging from a nail. The thing was just a rough casting in base metal with a red glass bead surrounded by a circle of half moons, and it reminded him of a horse brass, which was probably correct. The present-day thieves had not considered the little medallion worth removing, but Harry knew the original purpose of horse brasses and his thoughts began to race.

Imagination and curiosity had given him courage. He had seemed to hear Miriam's voice urging him on, and a name in the Holtby family tree had made him shrug aside his fears and enter the house. He was still afraid, still horrified by the pathetic figure lying on the couch, but he had begun to feel that he was in no personal danger – not at the moment. The other imagined voice had said that the guardian of the treasure was free. If that was true, four modern deaths could be explained, and the people who had condemned a child to living burial had had a practical motive for their act.

Four deaths within the last two days – how many in the past? What was the mysterious malady that had ravaged the area after Sir Arthur Holtby's return home with a foreign wife, and why had the mason and the last owner of the house killed themselves?

And how many deaths might occur in the near future? Harry slipped the disc into his pocket. The explanation occurring to him seemed completely illogical and irrational and he hardly liked to consider it. But there were two possible sources of information which might reveal whether he was on the right lines or a superstitious fool.

He thought of Miss Vallance's bandaged face while he

picked up the mask again and sniffed at the eye-shield. No odour remained, but a few grey shreds which could be dried herbs still clung to the leather, and they suggested his theory was at least possible.

Harry was not a religious man nor a sentimental man, but he crossed himself and laid the two hands beside their wrists before he left the room. Hands which Naureen Carlin had severed to remove the dead girl's bracelets. Bracelets which had made Naureen repeat a nursery rhyme when she was dying. He also eased the fireplace back into position. The demolition workers would open the cell soon enough, but it seemed proper to give the corpse a little more privacy.

Then he turned and ran. He ran down the long winding corridor with his feet crunching the sand and resounding from the bone-dry floorboards. He ran past the window through which the gang had entered the house and left with the fruits of their raid. He ran across the hall and into the porch with his heart and brain racing, and his fingers trembled as he struck a match to examine the second source of information.

The evidence was there at the foot of the carved slab, just as he had feared and suspected it might be, and he hurried on. On up the rutted drive to the main road and Delford village. On to find transport back to London. On to visit the most important item of the Holtby collection. Not silver, not gold, not precious stones, but power. A guardian which had defied death and was on the rampage.


'Rings on her fingers and bells on her toes.' The rhyme had been one of the last things to trouble Naureen Carlin, and its refrain had kept running through Miriam's head after she died. She had lost her patient, the Pentothal-strychnine injection had accelerated the death process and all she had been able to tell Harry were jumbled words and phrases which would probably be of little assistance to him. Miriam's sense of inadequacy and frustration had been like a physical illness when the sheet was finally drawn over Naureen's face. She had failed to help her and felt more and more certain that no doctor, or reporter, or policeman could ever discover the truth, though a priest might.

But, although one patient was dead, there were plenty of others in need of help and Miriam had been kept busy throughout the day. A shop-lifter and an alcoholic. An eight-year-old bed-wetter whose parents had tried to cure him by tying his sodden pyjamas around his face whenever a lapse occurred. A young theological student who had roasted his hand over a gas stove in the belief that he was Archbishop Cranmer. An insurance clerk; the indulgent father of a large and happy family who now sat hunched in a chair, quite motionless apart from the tears trickling down his cheeks. Why had such a man bought his children a puppy and then made them look on while he strangled it?

None of these people were suffering as badly as Naureen Carlin had done, but they kept Miriam fully occupied and it was evening before she took a break in the canteen, and thought of another person in need of help. Susan Vallance practising her role with an intensity that suggested drugs or acute schizophrenia. An intensity which would stimulate the adrenal system as it had done in Naureen's case. No human being could sustain such emotion for long and Miss Vallance had a weak heart already. Without tranquillizers or self control she'd be a wreck before the final curtain.

But Dame Susan had rejected help and nothing could be done for her. She was a free agent and if she wished to kill herself in the interest of art, that was her own business. Miriam picked up the early edition of an evening paper someone had left lying on the table and tried to relax. She glanced at the headlines which were devoted to a cabinet meeting on unemployment, started to turn to the crossword and as she did so a name seemed to leap out at her eyes as one had leapt out at Harry's in the porch at Flethertarn Hall.

Trenton – Paul Trenton. The news item was only thirty words long, and misleading as well as short. It merely stated that the man had died of a drug overdose in Newbury Circus tube-station and did not mention that the drug in question was a conventional form of sleeping pill. An omission which made Miriam get up from the table and hurry out of the canteen to find a phone booth.

Miriam had never accepted Harry's early theory that some secret preparation which left no trace in the system might be responsible for Naureen Carlin's guilt and terror. A pep-up which first stimulated the subject into unaccustomed activity and then caused complete mental breakdown. She had believed Miss Vallance's denial that Trenton had given her chemical aids to improve her performance, but she wasn't sure now. The paper definitely stated that a drug overdose killed Trenton, and Trenton was the link between Starr and the Carlins and Susan Vallance. The woman must be told about Trenton's death and warned of the danger she was in if she had received any pills or injections from him.

'I want to speak to Dame Susan Vallance please.' Miriam had dialled the number and a voice repeated it. 'My name is Dr Stanford.'

'I'm afraid I can't help you, madam.' She had expected to hear one of the maids, but the voice was male. 'This is Miss Vallance's answering service and she is accepting no calls or messages at present.'

'I'm sorry, Doctor.' Miriam had told him that her business was urgent, but the man remained adamant. 'Those are my instructions, but if you will give me your number I will tell Miss Vallance you called after she returns home from the theatre.'

After she returns? Miriam replaced the receiver. Susan Vallance was due on stage in an hour and a half and she must have given the answering service their instructions so that no telephone bell would disturb her concentration on the part. The man might have more accurately said, 'if she returns,' because 'if' was the operative word.

If the symptoms she and Harry had witnessed last night had been produced by drugs, Trenton must have given Susan Vallance a second supply for the coming performance and she had an unstable heart. The Pegasus was a large theatre and several thousand people might see a frenzied maniac die on the stage for their entertainment.

Susan Vallance could already be past help, but that exhibition had to be prevented. Miriam left the phone booth. Miss Vallance must be warned and a personal visit was the only way to deliver the warning. She hurried to the exit with the nursery rhyme lilting in time to her steps. 'Rings on her fingers and bells on her toes – She shall have music wherever she goes.'

# Chapter 16

'In your opinion there is no link between the material and spiritual worlds, Padre?' Harry leaned forward on his seat in the railway compartment. 'Does that mean you deny the existence of the supernatural?'

'Not at all, sir.' The train roared into a tunnel, making speech impossible, and Canon Archibald Nock pondered Saint Paul's words on charity till the noise subsided. A hard text to live with, he thought, and without it he would probably have moved to another carriage. His travelling companion was proving himself a most tiresome fellow and had badgered him with questions since they left Delford.

'For instance, as a Christian I am expected to believe in transubstantiation. That during the mass the wine and wafers actually do become the blood and body of Our Lord, but relics are quite a different matter.' Nock spoke nervously. The questioner was an untidy young man with dust on his clothes and a bruise on his forehead and clearly in a state of excitement. He had come rushing down the platform just as the train was due to pull out, passed the door of his compartment and then turned back and climbed in beside him.

'We live in a scientific age and such things should be taken with a grain of salt.' The canon tried not to yawn. He was extremely tired, having just presided over a long and rancorous debate by the Delford Women's Institute at the invitation of the vicar, and had missed the train he'd intended to catch.

He would have to go straight from the London terminus and take evensong without stopping for a cup of tea, and the one consolation had been finding a quiet seat to himself. Now this wretched individual was subjecting him to an interrogation.

'If all the supposed fragments of the true cross lying about in Spain and Italy were gathered together they'd probably fill a fair-sized timber yard.' Nock wished he was not wearing a dog-collar. He believed in the dignity of his cloth, and would have been offended if one of his parishioners addressed him as Archie, but that strip of cellulose could lead to unwelcome encounters at times.

'I was referring to genuine relics, Padre.' Nock had been right in blaming the collar for his plight. A loudspeaker was announcing the train's departure when Harry reached the station and he had also hoped to find a quiet seat in which to marshal his thoughts. But the sight of a clergyman had suggested that professional information was available and he'd decided to pick Nock's brains. 'If a piece of wood had actually been part of Christ's cross, wouldn't you expect it to have magical properties?'

'A difficult point – very difficult.' Nock was in a predicament. He didn't want to upset his companion, who might be a religious maniac ready to turn violent if he received answers which annoyed him, and he was in two minds on the subject. His mature intellect assured him that no such properties existed, but in his youth he had been fascinated by the occult, and that fascination remained.

'I suppose it's a matter of faith, though that has become rather a dirty word, and the modern term is psychosuggestion.' He risked a faint smile. 'The people who go to Lourdes to be cured believe that they will be cured and some of them are. Their hopes produce a bodily reaction to combat illness.'

'Then the water of Lourdes has no intrinsic healing quality?' If Nock was tired Harry was exhausted. Not by the long run to the station, though that had taxed him for a while. The mummified body and the theory it had aroused seemed to have drained his brain, and he felt like a punch-drunk boxer reeling against the ropes. 'When you baptize a child, is the water ordinary chlorinated $H_2O$?'

'Holy water has been blessed by a priest. The chemical formula does not change, but if the priest's authority stems from God, a mystical change is added by his blessing.'

Priestly authority! Nock lowered his face feeling sudden envy towards former clerics. In earlier ages that authority was accepted and a priest regarded with reverence. But today he had become a slightly comic figure whose main usefulness was that of a social worker. If only faith had not become a dirty word, he thought bitterly. If only science did not appear to show that the universe was governed by dull, rational laws. If only the mystery remained. When he was first ordained, Nock's own belief in the Gospels had been complete, but though his faith had dwindled over the years the questions had started to revive it. And, although the young man might be mentally unbalanced, it was unkind to dismiss him as a lunatic. He was a visionary longing for the assurances he himself had once possessed.

'My bishop is a modern churchman who would not approve of what I am going to say, and my intelligence has virtually rejected the possibility of a spiritual existence divorced from the flesh.' He raised his head and looked Harry in the eyes. 'But in my soul – my heart of hearts, I feel quite sure that certain material substances may possess qualities which cannot be explained by science. Powers of healing, exorcism and extreme longevity.'

'Please go on, Padre.' He had fallen silent and Harry prompted him. 'Can you think of any instances of longevity?'

'Several.' Nock's confession had embarrassed him for a moment, but he was starting to warm to the subject. 'Saint Veronica's veil is of dubious authenticity, but tests have shown that the Turin shroud dates from the beginning of the Christian era. Could any ordinary woollen garment have survived so long?

'One of the most convincing examples is the body of Saint Cuthbert, of Northumbria, who was buried in 687. The coffin was opened several times over the centuries and on each occasion the corpse was found to be free from decay. Almost a thousand years after the saint's death, a witness reported that his flesh remained "sound, sweet and flexible."

'But is anything wrong?' Nock had expected Harry to show interest but the reaction was much stronger than that. He had given a gasp and his face became ashen. 'Have I said something to distress you?'

'You have horrified me, Padre.' Harry had received the information which he'd dreaded to hear and his worst fears were confirmed. 'You consider that God can suspend the laws of nature and lodge benevolent powers in lifeless objects.

'So, what about the enemy?' Harry drew the little medallion from his pocket and stared at the red bead and the circling moons. He knew what was causing the outbreak of death and mania, he knew the nature of the guardian, or rather guardians, but he had no idea how their bent crusade could be halted. 'Isn't it possible that Satan may also have endowed inanimate objects with forces of destruction?'

# Chapter 17

Miriam had been delayed. On reaching the hospital parking lot she'd found that her car was hemmed in by a disreputable van embellished with slogans and football club stickers and it took the public address system some time to locate the student responsible and get him to remove his vehicle. Now the traffic was holding her back and she fumed and fretted and constantly looked at the dashboard clock. The curtain was due to rise on *Our Lady of Pain* at 7.30 and it was a quarter to the hour already. If Miss Vallance was not feeling too ill to appear she might be on her way to the Pegasus by now and Miriam considered driving there and waiting for her, and then decided to stick to her first plan. The theatre was not far from Miss Vallance's flat and the actress was under great stress. In Miriam's opinion it was unlikely that she would leave home until the last moment.

Almost there though. Ignoring a blast of protesting horns she swung in front of a taxi and an oncoming bus and accelerated down a side street. The grandiose façade of Lethbridge Mansions was straight ahead and she drew into the courtyard, lifted her medical bag from the seat and jumped out, slamming the car door behind her.

There was no porter in evidence to tell her if Miss Vallance had already left and Miriam hurried to the lift, considering her approach as the cage slid smoothly up. 'Paul Trenton is dead, Susan. He killed himself with an overdose of the same drug that he gave you, and it is imperative that you accept help. I've brought tranquillizers with me and a prophylactic to prevent arterial damage and you must let me give you an injection here and now.'

An unimpressive approach, and she was probably too late to deliver it. Miriam had left the lift and rung the bell of the flat three times. The door had a glass panel and a light glowed behind it, but there was no response to her calls. With two maids in residence that seemed odd, though not so very odd. Susan Vallance was a martinet, but she liked the applause of her minions as well as the general public. She must have given the girls seats for the play and the three of them had gone off to the theatre together.

'Don't just stand there. Nobody can hear you.' Miriam's common sense prompted her to leave. The flat appeared to be deserted, no sound or movement came from behind the panel, and her only course was to go to the Pegasus and try to reason with Miss Vallance in her dressing-room. If Susan Vallance was capable of reason, of course. She might already be a sick and incoherent woman.

'Go to the theatre, damn you.' Miriam tried to turn away from the door, but her body refused to obey her. The leg muscles seemed to be paralysed, goose pimples were rising on her skin and her feet were rooted to the floor. She stared at the door and the cause of her indisposition became clear. An envelope was wedged in the letter slot. A thick, buff envelope, probably containing a catalogue or a brochure, and a smell was coming through the gap it created. Two smells joined into one and each was familiar to her. Smells associated with illness and pain and death, which she had often experienced in the hospital and twice on the scene of motor accidents.

But they were not associated with luxury Mayfair flats, and as Miriam recognized them she lowered the bag and reached for a shoe. All her sense of responsibility and self-preservation had vanished, just as Harry's had done when he decided to impersonate a priest, steal a map and enter an empty house.

Without any thought of the consequences, she slipped off the shoe, raised it over her shoulder and slammed the heel against the panel.

An insane solution, but the only one which fitted the known facts. Harry was also late and like Miriam he cursed London's rush hour as the doors of the tube train opened again and more city commuters squeezed into the crowded carriage.

Mental illness produced by abnormal will-power and transmitted by rays. A disease which multiplied squeamish aversions into terror. Results: madness, suicide, heart-failure. While Harry was talking to Canon Nock in the main-line train he had felt sure that the theory must be correct. Now, crammed between two bowler-hatted businessmen and two girls who were discussing the sexual shortcomings of their office manager, he was less convinced. In spite of the facts, it was hard to believe that such a thing existed in the twentieth century.

'The force in question was once feared throughout the entire Western world,' Nock had said. 'Even today it is still regarded as factual in the Middle East and in many rural European communities. As you say, horse brasses were originally charms to protect the animals that wore them.' The canon had examined the medallion and handed it back to Harry. 'Being one of man's most valuable possessions, the horse was a popular victim.'

'When we was checking the Cohen-Huxtable contract he pressed himself right up against me, Marge.' The train had finally clicked off down the tunnel and the girls' voices interrupted Harry's thoughts. 'A real dirty old goat he is.'

'You don't have to tell me that, Doreen. He asked me for a dance at the last office party. Rather pleased I was, because I was new to the firm and imagined he was just being kind and taking a fatherly interest. But after a few steps I started to feel him through my skirt. Feel *it*, if you know what I mean.'

'I know all right, Marge, and how disgusting in a man of his age.' The first girl was applying her lipstick while she talked and Harry noticed that she wore a matching shade of nail varnish; amber. The walls of the cell at Flethertarn Hall might have been much the same colour before the paint faded, and he concentrated on what Canon Nock had told him.

'The Gorgon story probably belongs to the same tradition.' The canon had clearly given the matter a deal of study. 'The common belief today is that Medusa was a monstrosity. A woman so hideous that the mere sight of her could turn men to stone – strike them rigid with horror. But many classical sculptures and bas-reliefs depict her as being extremely beautiful, apart from the serpents forming her hair. If that was the case, how did she manage to produce such revulsion?'

A monstrosity! The Holtby legend suggested that the child had been hideously deformed, but his own eyes had told Harry that that was not true. Though wizened by time and mutilated by human hands she had been physically normal when alive.

The train had stopped, Doreen's lips had been coated to her satisfaction, and Harry remembered something else the canon had told him just before they reached London. 'In Arabic countries certain shades of red and brown are believed to form protective screens to ward off an attack.'

'My wife made me get tickets for that.' One of the bowler-hatted men nodded at an advertisement on the station wall. 'We're going next week, worst luck. Don't like the theatre, and I can't stand Susan Vallance at any price.' He grimaced sourly. '*Our Lady of Pain*, indeed. A perverse title and I gather the play lives up to its name. All about some crazy woman who murdered a lot of girls in Hungary. Give me a musical or a good revue any day.

'Still, the missus is set on seeing it, and I suppose we must please the ladies, more's the pity.' He snorted and opened his paper at the stock-market prices.

Aversion turning to disgust – disgust to terror – terror to the unendurable. Harry tried to imagine the emotions Starr and the Carlins must have experienced at the end of their lives, and he considered his personal aversion; earwigs. How would he feel if he was naked and paralysed and the creatures were crawling over him. Little yellow bodies zigzagging across his chest. Tiny feet pattering up his neck towards their destination. A tickling sensation when the goal was reached. Agony as their teeth started to gnaw at his brain.

Yes, that would drive him insane and make death a welcome visitor, and Harry suddenly remembered a more recent outbreak of group mania than the Flagellants and the Mad Dancers of the Middle Ages. About twenty-five years ago, he couldn't recall the exact date, the inhabitants of a French village had become deranged. They experienced visions and delusions of persecution in which they were pursued by monstrous animals and balls of fire. Their terror was so great that squads of extra police were needed to restrain them, there were several suicides and many of the survivors never regained full mental health. The phenomenon might have been caused by the presence of the drug, *ergot*, in a consignment of infected grain, but the mystery had never been completely solved. Could that French village have provided a minor preview of what might be about to happen in London?

'Fool – damn fool. Forgot danger – Couldn't see to work – took them off.' Those were a few of Trenton's last words and he had had a pair of tinted sun-glasses in his pocket. Were their lenses the same colour as Doreen's nail varnish? Harry wondered. A shade of reddish brown believed to ward off the transmitters of fear.

If so, he needed such protection himself and it was available. The girl had replaced the lipstick and her handbag had a faulty catch. Through the gap Harry could see a little ornamental bottle and he edged closer to his companions as the

train lurched along the rails. Doreen and Marge were still occupied with the manager's shortcomings, the businessmen
were discussing a share issue, and the risk of detection was
slight. His fingers slid into the bag and he drew out the bottle
and placed it beside the medallion in his pocket. Another theft,
a further misdemeanour, but so what, when the stakes involved were enormous? Many people had died in the past and
before long the death roll might reach epidemic proportions.

'Ah, here's my station, Smithers, so I must love you and
leave you.' The wheels were grinding to a halt and one of the
bowler hats folded his paper. 'If we don't meet before your trip
to the theatre, have a thundering good time.' He grinned with
friendly malice. 'I know you're a ruddy Philistine, but a bit of
culture never harmed anyone.'

'Thanks for nothing, Lazenby.' Smithers snorted again.
'Never mind my lack of culture, just keep your fingers crossed
over that Osprey Oil issue. Christ knows how the shares will
go.'

Christ knows! Lazenby had marched off, the doors were
closing, but the flippant phrase still rang in Harry's ears and
he wished he had fully confided in Nock and asked the canon
to join forces with him. It was almost certain that Smithers
would be spared his theatrical ordeal, because the play would
only run for one night, and Christ did know. He knew how to
cure disease, just as his enemy, the Sower of Tares, knew how
to spread pestilence.

The first entry on the stone slab which aroused Harry's suspicions stated that Arthur Holtby had married a certain Christine Battery, and the Anglicized spelling had not confused him
for long. Miss Nevern had said that a Polish version of Christine was Krisia, and Sir Arthur's foreign bride was the one that
got away.

Krisia Bathori, the sister of Countess Elizabeth Bathori-
Nadasdy, and it was not Dracula but the countess who originated the vampire legend. Werewolf, sadist, mass murderess
and worshipper of human blood . . . Our Lady of Pain.

# Chapter 18

Three blows had shattered the panel and the glass fell inwards. Miriam inserted a hand, turned the spring lock and opened the door.

Chloroform! The hallway was heavy with its odour and she hesitated on the threshold. Outside her own profession few people used anaesthetics for honest purposes and an intruder must have entered the premises. The sensible course was to go and find help, and if the other smell had not been present she would have done that. But the salty, reeking tang mingled with the drug suggested that Miss Vallance and her staff might be in urgent need of medical attention and there was no time to lose. She replaced her shoe, lifted the bag from the floor and walked across the hall.

The whole flat was brightly lit and nothing had been disordered in the room where Miss Vallance had given her party. A log fire glowed cheerfully in the grate and a standard lamp shone beside a glass-fronted cabinet filled with Spode china. In another cabinet Dame Susan's collection of Georgian silver was undisturbed. If a burglar had been present he must have overpowered the flat's occupants and made off empty-handed by the back door when he heard the panel break.

Unless the man was interested in more portable property than china and silver and was at work elsewhere. Miriam edged quietly across the room and down a passage. At each step the smell of chloroform increased and when she reached the main bedroom its source was apparent. A wad of cotton wool and an unstopped bottle lay on the dressing table.

Not robbery then. Other items on the table proved that. An open jewellery case with three rings and a brooch and a string of pearls strewn around it. Miss Vallance must have been selecting the ornaments she would wear for the theatre when something disturbed her.

Something – someone? Miriam had heard a movement and she crept over to the bedside telephone. The intruder was still on the premises and she had to get help. Though the answering service was not putting calls through, the exchange could be contacted and she lifted the instrument and then dropped it as though the plastic body was red hot.

The sound was not being made by any intruder and it was very close to her. A steady patter like water dropping from a blocked gutter or a leaking tap, like the slow tick of a clock. A noise without threat or menace in itself, but joined with the smells it suggested pain and mutilation and possible death. Blood dripping from a wound.

There was a door to the left of the bed and Miriam crossed towards it. Three victims of an attack must be behind that door. Two of them probably rendered unconscious by the chloroform and in no danger, while the third might have put up a fight and be badly injured. A tragic possibility, but not a personally frightening one, because the assailant must have fled when he heard her break the panel.

Yes, he must – must have left. Miriam reassured herself successfully, and she felt no fear as she grasped the doorknob, and she was quite calm when she pulled the door open. But when she saw what it had concealed she reeled back; numb, paralysed, too frightened to open her mouth and scream.

A thing from Room One Hundred and One was looking at her and its face was upside-down.


Trenton dead! The woman had also seen a newspaper, but her partner's death did not surprise or sadden her. Paul Trenton had ceased to be of use to her and he would have had to die, or been made to die shortly, in any event. His premature end merely meant that her abilities were not selective, but she had suspected that might be the case.

Trenton dead – Fleance fled. The woman was a Shakespearian scholar and an incident from *Macbeth* occurred to her as she dropped the paper into a litter bin. What she had learned was a disappointment but not a real setback and she strolled on through the evening crowds. People going home after a hard day at the office or the factory. People flocking in from the suburbs to visit theatres and cinemas and restaurants. People filling in time and meditating as she was doing. People . . .

Tired people who had had to work late. 'Sorry, Smith, but the board needs that schedule tomorrow and you'll just have to stay on and finish it.'

Tired, cheerful people heading for the pubs and a well-earned pint for the road. 'Who gives a bugger about the extra hours, mate? Think about the extra lolly.'

Tired, irritable, unwilling people, who had been forced away from the telly and their firesides. 'It may be a good show, darling, but two journeys to town in one day are a bit much.'

People! The woman wandered aimlessly through the streets. Now and again she glanced at shop windows, but her main interest was on her fellow pedestrians. People . . . Clerks and company directors – bank managers and typists – Solicitors and labourers and property-speculators. The world and his wife – Uncle Tom Cobley and all – Rich man, poor man, beggar man, thief. People – people too tired and preoccupied with their own insignificant lives to give her the attention which was her right – Bloody people. Their faces were blurred, but she could hear them and smell them and feel them brush past her, and another passage from *Macbeth* crossed her mind. 'Where hast thou been, Sister?'

She smiled and whispered the reply through the veil screening her mouth. 'Killing swine.'

Frenzy produced by drugs or over-involvement in a theatrical role – reincarnation – diabolical possession. Miriam stood in the doorway of Miss Vallance's bathroom quite unable to look away from the things above the bath.

The Countess Bathori had murdered six hundred and fifty children and young women and her punishment had been a hellish one. No light, no sound, and a cell so cramped that she could not sit nor stand nor lie down. The extraordinary feature was that her body had endured such conditions for almost four years. Was it possible that her spirit had survived the centuries and was still at work?

The bathroom had a high ceiling and a hook had been screwed into one of its joists. A light block and tackle device was attached to the hook and the naked bodies of Miss Vallance's maids were suspended over the bath by their heels. One of them had long hair which drifted like underwater seaweed in a breeze from a half-open window and obscured her face and neck, but the other girl was short-haired and the cause of their death was apparent. Small incisions had been made in their throats and they had died slowly like lambs ritually slaughtered before a rabbi. Scarlet drops were still dripping into the congealed blood that covered the base of the bath, and the room stank like an abattoir.

Where was the woman now? Miriam forced her eyes towards a shower cabinet and she saw that its floor was wet and a damp towel hung over a rail. Miss Vallance had relived her heroine's orgy and then washed the blood from her body and prepared to get ready for the theatre, as though nothing out of the way had happened. Like many split personalities she had probably forgotten the incident once the door closed on her victims, though she might have wondered why they were not in attendance to help her dress.

Drugs – obsession with a character study – reincarnation – possession. Once again Miriam considered the possibilities, and she remembered the bandaged face turned towards the imaginary judges and the scream that had rung out when they passed sentence. Had the spirit of a long-dead murderess entered her soul as a demon named Legion entered the beasts of the Gadarenes?

But the answer to the first question was obvious. Sick or possessed, conscious or oblivious of what she had done, Dame Susan would be at the theatre determined to give the performance of her lifetime.

A performance which must not take place. Miriam turned and made for the telephone, and a clock beside the bed showed that in less than half an hour the auditorium would fall silent and the curtain start to rise. At first, the stage would be in complete darkness, then a light glow to show Miss Vallance stationed before a window. A tiny light slowly becoming brighter and brighter till its beam was almost unbearable and the actress swung round and faced her audience.

The curtain must not rise. For no logical reason, Miriam somehow knew the play had to be stopped and Miss Vallance kept off the stage. But what was the best way to stop it? If she called the police, several minutes would pass before they reached the flat and several more before they examined the evidence and took action. Would it be better to telephone the Pegasus and explain the situation to the manager or Patricia Nevern before contacting the police?

No, they'd never believe her and it had to be the police. Miriam dialled the emergency service and then froze. She was not alone and footsteps were coming towards her. Slow, cautious footsteps which might belong to a porter or a neighbouring tenant who had seen the broken door panel and decided to investigate.

They didn't though. The footsteps were uncertain as well as cautious and she heard a thud as their owner stumbled against a piece of furniture. A blind or blindfolded person was crossing the hall and she was wrong. Susan Vallance had not left for the theatre and Miriam hurried over to the dressing-table, poured more chloroform on to the cotton wool pad and prepared to defend herself against a crazed killer.

'Can you hear me, caller?' She had laid the phone on the bed and the operator's voice was loud and urgent. 'Which service do you want and from where are you speaking?'

'I want . . . I want help, of course.' Miriam screamed the request, because the footsteps had stopped and a shadow darkened the doorway. She drew back with the saturated pad in her hand and then dropped it and sobbed with relief.

She had expected to see the bandaged face of Susan Vallance but it was Harry Clay who stood before the door and Miriam ran towards him with arms outstretched and tears coursing down her cheeks. The feeling of comfort and relief made her feel that his arrival was like a gift of God, but the feeling vanished abruptly when she reached him, and she drew back in panic.

Harry Clay's appearance had altered. He had the set, lifeless expression of a blind man and his eyes were out of focus. Red, inhuman eyes – the eyes of a satyr.

## Chapter 19

'What the hell's delayed her?' Jonathan Mandel, the producer of *Our Lady of Pain*, raised his watch to his ear in the hope that something had gone wrong with the works and it was gaining badly. But the tick was as slow and steady as usual and he turned to Patricia Nevern in consternation. 'Got the time on you, Pat?'

'Yes, twenty-eight minutes to the curtain.' The writer's mannish cynicism had vanished and she was as concerned as Mandel. 'Christ! Don't tell me the old bitch has got an attack of nerves and won't be coming. If we have to open with June Ronson in the lead they'll crucify us.' Miss Nevern was terrified by the possibility and her fears were justified. Every seat in the Pegasus had been sold, every critic who mattered would be present and a box had been reserved for a royal party. The majority of the audience had only a vague idea what the play was about and their interest was centred on the star. They wanted to witness either Miss Vallance's triumphant comeback or another fiasco which would finish her for good and all. An announcement that her understudy was to take the main role would be received with fury.

'I just don't understand it, Pat. It's quite out of character.' They were stationed at the top of an iron staircase above the stage door and Mandel's hand clutched the banister like a claw. He was beside himself with worry because punctuality was one of Dame Susan's virtues and over the years her first-night arrivals had developed into a set ceremony. At exactly three-quarters of an hour before the performance was due to begin, her Rolls-Royce drew up before the main entrance of the theatre where the manager and his uniformed staff were assembled like a guard of honour. When the car door was opened for her, the great lady would step out, bow regally to the welcoming committee and then take the manager's arm and be led to the green room where she drank a glass of champagne with the rest of the cast and the senior technicians before going to dress.

But there would be no such ceremony tonight. The foyer was crammed already, the uniformed attendants were ushering the audience to their seats, and the other actors and actresses were dressed and made up.

'I can't understand it.' Mandel repeated himself in desperation. 'We both know how much this play means to Susan, how fascinated she's been by the part, so what's come over her? The role has caused her a lot of nervous strain, but that's understandable, and she was fine at the dress rehearsal. Really splendid, and I told her she had nothing to worry about.'

'So did I, Jonathan, but did she believe us?' Patricia Nevern was staring down the stairs in the hope of seeing the stage door open. 'Susan's scared to death of a second flop and in my view it's quite on the cards that she's in a state of collapse or having hysterics.'

'Ah, there you are, Nola.' A small, mousey woman had coughed to attract their attention and Miss Nevern swung round. 'Did you manage to get through?'

'I'm afraid not. The answering service still won't put through any calls, though I told the man how urgent it was.' Mrs Nola Frane had been Dame Susan's dresser for ten years and she was equally bewildered. 'I'm worried – worried stiff. It's not like Madam to be late. I've never known it happen all the time I've been with her, and something must be really wrong. Maybe she's had a motor accident on the way. Perhaps her heart's played up again and she's ill.'

'A motor accident's unlikely. Her flat's only a mile or two away and that chauffeur she uses drives like a snail. If there'd been a minor bump she would have taken a taxi.' Patricia Nevern looked at her watch and turned to Mandel. 'In any event you'd better tell June Ronson that she may be playing the countess.'

'Miss Ronson will do no such thing, Jonathan.' The words came from half way down the staircase and for a moment none of them recognized the speaker. 'The girl is a ham and quite unfit to take the lead in a village-hall pantomime.' Dame Susan's voice was as commanding as ever, but her appearance had baffled them. She normally arrived for her first nights in full evening dress, but now she wore a simple linen suit and a page-boy hat with a veil. A pair of glasses behind the veil heightened the disguise.

'The fact that I am slightly late and decided to dispense with the ceremony and champagne need not worry you, Patricia, and I am perfectly well, though your concern for my health is touching, Nola.' She bowed to Mandel and Miss Nevern as she mounted the stairs and laid a hand on Mrs Frane's arm. 'I am now going to dress, and will see you on stage, Jonathan.

'This building is like a second home to me, Nola.' Susan Vallance had often appeared at the Pegasus and she looked nostalgically around the dressing-room. 'I got my first real chance here; Helen of Troy in Marlowe's *Doctor Faustus.* Lovely, sensual Helen with "a face that forced a thousand shits to brain the brainless nits of Ilium."' Dame Susan laughed at the misquotation as she crossed to the dressing-table. 'And after *Doctor Faustus* came *Hedda Gabler* and *Tamburlaine* and *The Way of the World.* Then *Mother Courage* and that Shakespeare season which ran for a year; Cleopatra and Regan, Rosalind and Lady Macbeth and Portia.

'All triumphs, Nola. All performances that made theatrical history, and how one person must have envied them.' She looked at her make-up box on the table. 'A razor – a razor-blade hidden in a stick of eye shadow. I wonder if the man or woman who put it there will be watching me tonight.

'Finally, *Saint Joan* and humiliation.' She sat down and stared at the mirror through her veil. 'Do you remember my humiliation, Nola? Can you still hear those boos and catcalls and slow handclaps? I certainly can and the memory will never leave me.'

'I try to forget them, madam.' The woman had already put out Miss Vallance's costume and was waiting to start work. 'And so should you, because there'll be no boos or catcalls tonight, and it's the curtain calls you'll have to worry about. They'll cheer themselves hoarse when the play's finished.'

'Thank you for your confidence, my dear.' Miss Vallance laid her handbag on the table. 'Though we've been together a long time, Nola, I don't believe I've ever considered your feelings towards me and I want to ask you a question. Were you really worried when you thought I might be ill or had had a car accident?'

'Of course I was worried.' Mrs Frane blushed in embarrassment. 'I was scared stiff and that's only natural. Why, I've worked for you for donkey's years.'

'Only natural.' The lips curled behind the veil. 'Rather unnatural I would have imagined. My personality does not usually inspire affection.'

'It's not actual affection that I mean, madam.' The dresser spoke with her face lowered. 'Maybe association is the best way to describe what I feel about you. You're a great actress, one of the greatest the world has ever known, while I'm nothing – just a nobody.

'But working for you makes me feel I am somebody. When they cheer and clap you I somehow imagine that they're applauding me too. But when the opposite happened: when I listened to those bastards at *Saint Joan* I could have cut their tongues out.' She stepped forward to remove her employer's jacket. 'I'm sorry if that sounds impertinent, madam, but I can't help my feelings and what I've said is gospel truth. While I watch you from the wings this evening I'll almost start to believe that I'm up on the stage beside you.'

'You are not impertinent, Nola, and I'm extremely flattered.' Miss Vallance sounded pleased by the confession at first, and then her manner changed abruptly. 'No, on second thoughts I do find your identification with myself impertinent. Insolent

and presumptuous in the extreme, and you will not be watching me from the wings or anywhere else.' She pivoted round
on the dressing-table stool. 'I do not require your services any
longer, Nola. I intend to dress myself and you can leave the
theatre immediately.

'Don't argue with me, girl.' Mrs Frane had started to protest
and Susan Vallance's voice cracked like a whip. 'Go home, go
to a café or a pub or a cinema. Go anywhere you damn well
like, but leave this theatre because I can't stand having you near
me.

'That is an order, so stop snivelling and do what you're told.'
The woman was sobbing and Miss Vallance stood up. 'If you
are not out of this building in one minute I'll have you thrown
out.'

Poor little Nola, she thought as the door closed behind
her weeping minion. Poor, devoted, Mrs Nola Frane. Lucky
– lucky – Nola Frane. She slipped off her hat and her suit and
prepared to get ready.

Yes, lucky Mrs Frane. Dame Susan smiled as the parody
of a song occurred to her and she hummed the words
aloud. 'I care for nobody but myself, but Nola she cared for
me.'


'I tinted them with nail varnish, Miriam. I'll try to explain
why on the way to the theatre, but we must get there quickly.'
Harry had removed his contact lenses as soon as he realized
Miss Vallance had left, and after one glance at the bathroom he
had bustled Miriam out of the flat. Though the bodies hanging over the bath and the reek of blood and chloroform had
shocked him, he had not been surprised. In fact he had almost
expected to find something of the kind.

Because the basis of Satanism, as scores of witchcraft investigations have established, is destruction. Mental and physical
and spiritual murder, and the blood of children has always had
a mystical value for Satanists. Blood is the main element of the
eucharist Sabat and the aim of the devil-worshipper is to mock
God's creations. The quest for human blood inspired Gilles de

Rais and Dracula and Elizabeth Bathori, and Susan Vallance was following in their footsteps.

'The key word is darkness.' Harry continued his explanation as they hurried to the exit. 'The countess had to be arrested in the dark, and blindfolded before she could strike a light. The child whose body I found in Essex was not only locked up in a cell, a leather mask had been fixed to her head. It was essential that they did not look anyone in the face, you see.'

'Anyone they wished to harm.' Miriam groped for her car keys. 'Yes, I'm beginning to understand at last. Susan Vallance has not merely been possessed by an evil spirit, she has somehow adopted the powers of Countess Bathori.'

'Not of the countess, Miriam.' Harry climbed into the car beside her. 'Miss Vallance's gift originates from Elizabeth Bathori's sister, Krisia, who escaped from Hungary and came to England.

'I don't know how Susan Vallance and Trenton first met and joined forces; I haven't a clue what their original motivation was, or how they learned the nature of the guardians and decided to make use of them, but I am quite certain what happened afterwards. Starr and the Carlins were told that Krisia Bathori's jewellery had been hidden away with her child and given permission to take anything they wanted. But in return they had to deliver two apparently valueless objects to Trenton and the sight of those objects drove them insane.' Miriam had started the engine and Harry considered his conversation with Canon Nock as the car hurtled out into the street.

Material substances with the power to heal and exorcize and resist decay. The waters of Lourdes and Walsingham, the relics of martyrs, and the body of a saint that had remained pure and flexible after almost a thousand years. If one believed in such phenomena, and many sane people did, it was feasible to accept that other substances might have been endowed with malignant properties. Unholy relics with the power to kill and destroy and drive men mad.

A power that did not weaken after death. Harry slid a hand into his pocket and fondled the little medallion while he tried to explain the situation to Miriam. Metal and glass, he thought. Puny defences against the supernatural, and if they failed to protect him he might share the terrors that had turned Trenton's hair white and stopped Starr's heart beating. Nock had also said that Arab philosophers believed bright sunlight could ward off the forces of evil, but how could the sun penetrate a theatre?

'Don't talk. Just listen and get us to the Pegasus.' Miriam had turned her head to question him and Harry spoke sharply because she was weaving through the traffic like a stunt driver. 'There's no knowing how long the illness takes to develop. Probably the time-factors vary from individual to individual like the delusions which are created, but that's unimportant. Once infection takes place the subject has little chance of recovery and the important thing is to stop that play.'

'Which may not be necessary, Harry.' The theatre was in sight, but the street was blocked with stationary vehicles and Miriam slammed on her brakes. 'You believe that Naureen Carlin and the others went insane and died because they handled certain objects with magical properties. Well, Susan Vallance is insane, so isn't it probable that she also handled those objects and may be dying already?'

'Miss Vallance is not insane in the ordinary meaning of the term, Miriam, and she will be in normal physical health. The woman is an archetype – a personality who has rejoined her ancestors. The things from that cell cannot harm her because she is protected by a blood relationship.' The traffic jam was a solid mass, horns were honking impatiently and their blare made Harry recall Professor Brigham-Beer's booming tones. 'A name like Nally or Rally.' The professor must have been searching his memory for Valley, but he was still wrong and the inquirer had had a longer name. The last entry on the carved family-tree stated that a Miss Charlotte Holtby had married a man called Thomas Vallance and given birth to a daughter whom they christened Susan.

'I'll have to leave you, Miriam.' He reached for the door handle. 'When you get to the theatre, find the manager and tell him about the murdered girls in Miss Vallance's flat. He'll think you're crazy, but try to persuade him to hold back the play till he's spoken to the police. Do anything that comes to your mind. Create a scene, set the building on fire, but try to delay that curtain rising.

'And whatever happens, keep away from the auditorium.' Harry pulled Miriam towards him and kissed her on the mouth. 'If you value your life – if your soul means anything to you at all, don't look at the stage.' He opened the door and slid out, dodging between cars and buses and lorries to conduct an interview which might well be his last.

# Chapter 20

His press card and an assurance that the management had in-vited him to watch the play from the wings had got Harry past the door-keeper and when he reached the top of the iron stair-case it was clear that everybody was too preoccupied to notice his presence. The stage manager was giving a group of tech-nicians their final briefing. Jonathan Mandel was explaining some point to a portly actor wearing an ermine-tipped cloak and a velvet cap; probably one of the trial scene judges. Other members of the cast were chatting or silently going over their lines, but mercifully there was no sign of Miss Vallance and she must still be in her dressing-room.

Harry hesitated. A question would reveal him as an inter-loper and he'd have to find the room unaided. He walked across the rear of the curtained stage, stepping carefully over the light-ing cables. An operator was already in position at the control panel and one of the cables led to a carbon arc lamp positioned before a gap in the side drop. The prop which Patricia Nevern had described as second cousin to a small searchlight.

'Eight minutes, Miss Vallance.' A rap and a voice told Harry what he wanted to know and he turned down a narrow cor-ridor lined with doors. The voice belonged to an attractive girl wearing one of the shortest mini-skirts he had ever seen, and

the door she had knocked on had a star painted on the centre
panel. Having completed her summons she hurried back towards the stage and Harry stood aside to let her pass. Under
different circumstances the tiny skirt would have aroused
pleasant emotions, but not now. He was pretty sure what lay
behind the starred door, and his only emotions were fear, disgust and a sense of inadequacy. When the door opened, his
reason might be blasted, but there could be no going back.
However puny his defences and however great his fears the
challenge had to be faced. Harry slipped in his contact lenses,
clenched the metal disc in his left hand and reached for the
doorknob with his right.

Five minutes to go and the bells were ringing. Most of the audience had taken their places and the rest were filing in. They
moved to the front stalls where the critics were already seated.
They climbed to the circles and the boxes gay with evening
dresses. They toiled up to the gallery and the standing-room
section where beards and granny glasses and drab monkish
habits predominated. Every seat had been sold, soon the Pegasus would be packed from tier to tier, and almost everybody
had come to see the triumph or failure of an idol.

'What's your guess, Bill? Can the old girl make a comeback?'
The drama-critic of the *Weekly Diplomat* turned to his rival on
the *Sunday Comet*. 'I've heard she's been great at rehearsals, but
she'll have to be damn good to live that *Saint Joan* down.'

'Not having seen a rehearsal or been given a plot outline, I
haven't a clue, Robert.' The other man was looking at his programme. 'But, as it appears that the part's a sinister one, my
money is on a comeback. Susan was terrible as Joan; I've never
seen a worse, but there's no one to touch her when it comes to
the bloody-minded stuff. Remember her as Regan – remember
her Lady Macbeth and her Hedda Gabler; stupendous performances.'

'Agreed, but I still believe she'll go down tonight, so let's
have a fiver on it.' The *Diplomat's* representative grinned sourly.
'Maybe I'm just being bloody-minded myself, but I hope she

flops. I've disliked the woman since the first time I met her and I always shall.'

'A great actress – a great personality – how I envy her.' In the dress circle Miss Kathleen Lamley was trying to control her feelings. 'Think of the pleasure she gave you as Portia. Remember the night you went to Stratford and saw her Duchess of Malfi. Remember her as Cleopatra; you were so moved you had to stop yourself sobbing aloud.

'But if you'd had her chances, isn't it possible you might have done as well? If you'd had parents who could afford to send you to Cambridge . . . If you'd been trained by the C.U.D.S. and then at R.A.D.A. . . . If you hadn't had to leave school at fifteen and slave away in an office to support a sick mother, you might be in Susan Vallance's shoes right now.

'And if you were in her shoes, would you have behaved as she did?' A programme was open on Miss Lamley's lap and she frowned at a photograph of the actress. 'No, of course you wouldn't, Kathleen. You'd never have written that horrible, cruel note.' The letter in question had been delivered several years ago, but every word and punctuation mark, every stroke of the pen were riveted in her memory. 'Dame Susan Vallance thanks the secretary of the South Sheen Amateur Dramatic Society for their invitation to adjudicate in a one-act play competition between the said society and the Haverswyck Thespians. She must reluctantly decline, however, being a busy woman with no time to waste on amateurism in any of its tiresome forms.'

'Bitch . . . arrogant bitch.' Miss Lamley whispered to the face in the photograph. She was a kindly person who taught at the local Sunday school and collected industriously for a number of charities, but the letter had been addressed to her personally and she would never forgive its author. 'Bitch,' she repeated. 'Let the bitch flop, Lord God. If you believe in justice, God, give me the chance to boo her off the stage.'

'Bitch! What hell the bitch gave me! How I hated the bitch!'

Peter Rolfe was an actor who had been resting for a long time. He was too poor to afford a programme, but he needed no photograph to remind him of Susan Vallance. Her features were engraved in his memory.

'How I still hate her! How she humiliated me in *The Merchant*!' Rolfe had played the Prince of Arragon to Miss Vallance's Portia and it had been an unpleasant experience. He remembered the way she had constantly kept putting him off balance and insulting him. Sudden, unrehearsed moves across the stage – pauses at the end of his speeches as though she imagined he had forgotten his lines and left them unfinished. Whispered asides during his longest speech. 'They've miscast you, darling. You shouldn't be playing a prince, because you're a princess; a pansy, a pouf, a dear, little nancy boy.'

No, Peter Rolfe had not enjoyed *The Merchant of Venice* and his reprisal for the torment had not been as successful as he had hoped. 'How I hate her, and always will hate her,' he thought, sitting in the gods and waiting for the curtain to rise. 'If only that razor-blade I stuck in her eye shadow had cut a little deeper.'

'Keep your fingers crossed, Sarah love.' Sir Abraham Lazarus surveyed the audience from his box. The fact that the house was full pleased him, but he had invested a lot of money in the production and he was a very worried man. 'Though Mandel says the dress rehearsal went like clockwork, Susan Vallance is a temperamental bag of nerves and anything could happen. Bad thing temperament, Sarah. Nerves never bought no mink coats.'

'Stop fretting yourself, Abe.' Lady Lazarus's gold-plated opera-glasses were trained on the reviewers. The *Diplomat*'s critic had cracked a joke and his near neighbours were chuckling heartily. 'Them's the fellers that count and they all look happy enough.'

'Yes, smiling ain't they? Nice to smile it is, Sarah, so let's hope that they're still smiling when they write their notices.' He squeezed his wife's plump shoulder. 'Because I'll tell you this, love. If them boys stop smiling, you and I will stop eating.'

## Chapter 21

'What are you doing here, Nola?' Miss Vallance had heard the door open and assumed that her dresser had returned. 'I told you to leave the theatre, so why have you disobeyed my orders?' She snatched up her spectacles before swinging round on the stool. They had thick tortoiseshell frames and the lenses were tinted a light, reddish purple.

'You – how dare you?' She stood up as she recognized Harry. Apart from the glasses replacing the bandage she looked much the same as when he had last seen her, with a long, white robe and sandals on her feet. But the bright dressing-room lights and her stage make-up made her appear taller and even more formidable.

'Mr Clay, I am not in the habit of talking to reporters before opening nights, and your editor will hear about this intrusion.' She pointed to the door. 'Now, get the hell out of here.

'Are you deaf?' Harry had not moved and she stamped the carpet. 'I am due on stage in a few minutes, so get out.'

'You are not going anywhere near the stage.' Harry closed the door behind him. 'If the play is performed, which I doubt, an understudy will have to take the role of the countess, Miss Vallance. Or should I say, Christine Holtby, or Krisia Bathori?'

'You know?' She reeled back as though Harry had struck her and he saw that his suspicions were true. 'You discovered the connections?'

'I know almost everything, Miss Vallance. You are the lineal descendant of a monster. A vampire and a werewolf who escaped from Hungary and came to this country. I know why Elizabeth Bathori had to be blindfolded during her trial. I know what caused that outbreak of sickness when her sister arrived in Essex. I know why Krisia's daughter had to be locked away so that nobody could see her face.' Harry was gripping the metal disc so tightly that the rim was biting into his palm. 'They possessed the Evil Eye, didn't they? The power to create terror in the brain of an enemy . . . to spread death and mental disease through an act of concentration.

'The thieves removed the dead child's eyes for you and that destroyed them. The tissue was still alive, still able to transmit the hatred that girl felt towards the people who imprisoned her. The mere sight of her eye tissue is lethal.'

'You are perfectly correct, Mr Clay.' Susan Vallance literally spat out the name and saliva sprayed Harry's cheek. 'But as you are so well-informed, why did you come here? Don't you realize what will happen if I remove these glasses?'

'I know what might happen, because I witnessed Starr's death and Carlin's suicide.' A flicker of pain, physical pain, had crossed the woman's face and Harry felt slightly more confident. Miss Vallance had adopted elemental forces which were not subject to death or decay, but her own body was mortal. Her ancestry could protect her from the supernatural dangers, but what about the physical risks? Was it possible that the human and alien cell tissues were at war with each other? 'You may have the means to will my death, Dame Susan, but you are not leaving this room. I know what you intend to do when you reach the stage. You made that very clear long ago. "When you next see me I shall play a demon and tear your souls."'

'Three minutes, Miss Vallance.' The girl knocked on the door again. 'On stage in three minutes please.'

'Thank you.' The actress replied quite normally and smoothed back a lock of hair from her forehead. 'Mr Clay, you may be well-informed, but your use of the terms *concentration*, *will* and *intend*, shows that you do not know one important factor and neither did I till recently.' She lowered her face as though the lights troubled her.

'Power, that was what I wanted . . . what I craved for all my life. Power to destroy mockers and detractors, and one night I had a vision. A dream that told me where the seeds of power were hidden. Living cells which can lie dormant for centuries like certain types of bacilli and become active again when moisture or light revives them.' A hand crept towards the glasses and Harry knew that the challenge would soon begin.

'But there is no selectivity, no control, and the power belongs to its original owners. That is why Paul Trenton died. We both believed that the force could be harnessed after I received it and he dissolved the mummified tissue in a solvent, soaked lint with the liquid and bandaged the lint to my eyes. But he never guessed that that child's personality lives on and she wished to destroy him . . . to destroy every human being and everything that breathes. Even to destroy Me, Mr Clay . . . Susan Vallance who released her from the tomb.' Her accent suddenly became harsh and foreign and Harry raised his hand. 'Look at my daemons, peasant.

'No – no – please no.' As she removed the spectacles Harry held out the metal disc and she swung her face away from it and screamed. Three voices screamed. One was her own, one was thick and guttural and the other was a child's voice. An unhappy, frightened child locked away in a lonely prison. 'Let me out, Father. Please don't keep me here forever. You know I hate the heat of the sun, but the darkness is worse – far worse, and I'm so cold and wretched.

'Elizabeth and I were only girls when we made our bargain with Lucifer and I have never regretted that pact.' The second voice spoke and above the mouth Harry saw what Trenton's graft had done to her. The foreign cell tissue was stronger than her own and her eyes – her Gorgon's eyes were swelling. They were bulging out from the sockets, and he was quite certain that the same process would be taking place behind the skull when the brain had been penetrated. Miss Vallance was not merely spiritually possessed, the flesh of her ancestors was devouring her. He also knew that without the medallion and his tinted lenses the sight of those eyes would blast him.

'Clever, Mr Clay. You came prepared and I cannot harm you. You also know that I'm dying and I only realized that myself a few minutes ago.' She had read his thoughts and her normal voice returned. 'Yes, Susan Vallance will die soon, but what does death matter? My dream . . . my vision promised me joy; an eternity of bliss, and when I read that diary, when I guessed why my uncle had killed himself, I knew that that joy could be mine.

'Blood . . . blood.' She had broken off as though a gag had been pressed against her mouth and the guttural accents rasped out. 'How those sluts screamed when Elizabeth and I flogged them. We whipped them till their bodies were scarlet before we strung them up and then . . .' Miss Vallance's tongue licked her lips at the remembered pleasures of a dead woman. 'Then the blood really flowed. Warm, salt, refreshing blood. The restorer of beauty – the elixir of life – the very source of creation.

'We killed six hundred and fifty-two before anyone dared to lay a finger on us.' The deformed face creased with humour and though the nail varnish impaired Harry's sight he saw that the eyes were growing bigger as he watched them. 'People knew that looks really could kill.

'But at last they found the method to defeat us. While I was away from the castle, they drugged poor Elizabeth's wine and blindfolded her as she slept.' There was no humour in the face now, and anger darkened its features. 'Because of a few hundred worthless drabs they arrested my sister, the Countess Bathori, the niece of a king, and they walled her up in a tomb. But I escaped, and before I died I prayed to our master and he transferred his gifts to my child.

'Mr Clay, you have taken up too much of my time, and I must ask you to excuse me.' Music had started to play, a thudding overture based on a Bartok theme, and Miss Vallance spoke as though Harry was a casual visitor. 'The audience is waiting. Three thousand people who have paid money to see my performance, and some of them will be people who booed and jeered at me not so long ago. One of them may be the person who tried to blind me with a razor-blade and I do not intend to disappoint them.

'Please, Father . . . Please let me out. I couldn't help myself and I didn't mean any harm.' The child whimpered and tears ran from the monstrous things bulging from the eye sockets. 'Let me out into the light again.'

'For Christ's sake hurry up, Susan.' A man was hammering on the door. 'You should have been on stage two minutes ago.'

'I shall be with you directly, Jonathan.' She turned as if to check her make-up in the mirror. 'You were very clever to colour your contact lenses, Mr Clay, and realize that that talisman can defend you from the supernatural forces at my disposal.' She opened a drawer in the dressing-table and swung round quickly. 'It is no protection against cordite, however.

'You should thank me for an easy death, my friend.' Harry had toppled to the floor and she thought of the more sinister ways her audience would die. The overture had drowned the report of her .22 automatic, but the bullet had found its target and blood from Harry's forehead was soaking into the carpet.

'Goodbye, Mr Clay.' She laid down the little pistol, replaced her glasses and walked towards the door. An unholy trinity contained in the body of one person. The lethal eyes of a child, a demon's spirit and an artist's talent. The great dramatic talent of Miss Susan Vallance, D.B.E., one of the most accomplished performers in the world, who was about to reveal the worst things in the world. The varied inhabitants of Room One Hundred and One.


# Chapter 22


'You may be a doctor of medicine, madam, but you are clearly deranged.' The manager of the Pegasus was short both in stature and temper and his five-foot-two-inches quivered indignantly. 'You honestly expect me to postpone the play because of some cock-and-bull story that Miss Vallance is a murderer – a homicidal maniac. I've never heard anything so absurd in my life.

'Let go of my arm this instant, Dr Stanford.' Miriam had buttonholed him beside a door leading to the stalls and he tried to pull away from her grasp. Till a few minutes ago he had been in an optimistic mood, delighted with the full house and confident that *Our Lady of Pain* would have a long run. But all at once everything had started to go wrong. The curtain should have risen several minutes ago, the overture was approaching its climax for the second time and the audience becoming restive. Now this blasted woman had gone out of her mind.

'You must listen to me, Mr Chambers.' A commissionaire had given Miriam his name. 'What I've told you is the truth and Susan Vallance cannot be allowed on stage.'

'Will you release me, Doctor?' Chambers struggled to free himself again, but she still clutched his dinner jacket. 'Go to the police with your absurd notions, but leave me alone.

'Ah, Mabel and Joyce, come over here at once.' Two ush-erettes were approaching and he beckoned to them. 'Get this woman out of the theatre immediately and use force if neces-sary. She is mentally unbalanced and creating a disturbance.'

'Don't worry, I'll leave of my own accord.' Miriam relaxed her grip. The usherettes were hurrying to their superior's aid and they were both tall, heavily-built girls with no-nonsense faces who would dismiss her story as contemptuously as Chambers. Nobody would believe her, but though she couldn't blame them, the play had to be stopped.

'All right, luv.' The girls were used to dealing with difficult people and they spoke firmly but kindly. 'There's no need to make a scene, so come along quietly.'

'Hey, you can't go in there. Mr Chambers wants you off the premises.' Their hands shot out, but Miriam twisted past them and ran into the auditorium. The lights were dimming, the music had ended and the audience were tucking away pro-grammes and newspapers and clearing their throats before the curtain rose.

The rustling papers reminded Miriam of a gag which must have been used in a hundred cinema comedies till it became a cliché, and a typical fall-guy for Chaplin and Keaton and Harold Lloyd was on hand – an enormously stout man sitting in an aisle seat and folding a copy of the *Daily Globe*. Miriam had no idea that the man was John Forest, but he was the obvious target and she opened her handbag and dashed towards him. Before the usherettes could stop her she had flicked on her cigarette lighter and applied its flame to the newspaper.

He had fallen from a cliff, or a ladder, or a high building and he was lying on the ground. He'd been mugged in the street, or knocked down by a car, and he had to keep still because the concussion had blinded him.

But though help would arrive soon, he couldn't wait long. There was something he must do – something important. An appointment to be kept, a personality to be interviewed, an article to be written. If only he could remember what the assignment was.

'. . . a bit of culture will improve your mind, son.' A voice, John Forest's voice, joined the pounding noise in Harry's head, and he recalled the editor's instructions. He had to review a Shaw play starring an actress named Vallance – Dame Susan Vallance.

How could he? He was a crime reporter, not a critic, he knew nothing about the drama, and he was blind. All the same, the job had to be done, because it was dangerous to fall foul of Fatty Forest. If he let Forest down he'd probably end up on one of the *Globe*'s local papers writing about bishops and mayors and school buildings.

Harry took a deep breath and raised his hands to his eyes. His face was covered with some sticky substance and his fingers slipped before he gained the purchase he needed. But he succeeded at last and gave a sigh of relief as the light returned. His contact lenses were thickly coated with blood and some kind of varnish and he was not lying on the ground, but on a pile carpet. He staggered to his feet and tried to take in his surroundings.

Forest had told him to go to a theatre and it seemed that he was already there. Framed photographs and billboards on the walls and a mirror surrounded by strip lights suggested that he was in an actor's dressing-room and the face in the mirror belonged to an actor who had been made up for a *Grand Guignol* production. It took him some time to recognize the face as his own because a deep furrow ran across his temple, and his cheeks and jaws were dark with the congealing blood that had coated the lenses.

The room had a wash basin and he considered cleaning his face but decided against it. Water would reopen the wound and there was no time. He had to review a play, Forest would break him if he failed to do so, and he must find his way to the auditorium.

Harry noticed a horse brass lying on the floor beside his discarded lenses and an automatic pistol on the dressing table, but they were obviously theatrical props and unimportant. All that mattered was the play and he had to watch it from start to finish. He lurched out of the room, banging his head against the door post as he reached the corridor. Blood gushed from the opened wound, but that was equally unimportant, and he was still in time. The overture was booming away, the stage was in front of him and soon he would find people to direct him to his seat.

But the music stopped before he reached the end of the passage, the lights became fainter and fainter, and Harry halted in semi-darkness, hearing voices speaking in whispers, but not knowing where they came from.

'One sodding thing after another, Jonathan. First, *the great I am* arrives late and hangs about in her dressing-room till we think she's got stage fright. Then some nutty woman sets fire to a chap's newspaper. Wish us both luck, because I've got a hunch we'll need it.'

'Me too, Dave.' The second man raised his voice. 'We're ready, Susan, so get rid of those sun-glasses. And you can start the curtain, Clarke.'

Susan – Susan Vallance! Harry groped his way forward. Miss Vallance was the actress he had come to see and now he was seeing her. A tiny light had been directed through a gap in the scenery and her face was visible. Just a blurred image at first, but as the light increased and he drew nearer, memory came racing back and he knew what his assignment was.

Not to watch a play, but to defeat a demon. To fight an evil spirit that had resisted death and could drive men and women insane. The head beyond the gap was averted, but he knew that it belonged to a monster – a Gorgon who turned her victims to stone by imaginary horrors. Rats for Martin Starr, Fergus Carlin entwined by snake-like entrails, Paul Trenton's hair turning white because a dead man pursued him.

A Gorgon? The head was rising and Harry saw that the comparison was inapt. Medusa had had two eyes, but Susan Vallance possessed only one now. The foreign tissue had swollen into a single glittering Cyclops orb which was united across the bridge of her nose and dominated the whole face. She was probably in agony, but the will to destroy would not desert her and very soon that orb would swing towards the audience, because the curtain was up.

The men Harry heard speaking had moved away to the far side of the stage and the only person near to him was an electrician, who was seated before the lighting control panel holding a stop watch in his left hand and very slowly turning a knob with his right.

A knob – the knob of a dimmer switch – a rheostat – a sliding resistance to increase or decrease the current to the carbon arcs. The weapon Harry needed, because Patricia Nevern had said that the lamp was a dangerous prop and Arabic philosophers believed that the sun's rays could frustrate the powers of evil. No sunlight was present, but it was possible that a man-made substitute would do as well. Harry braced himself and stumbled towards the panel.

He was weak from the loss of blood and only half conscious. Without an accident he would probably not have reached his goal in time, and if he had done the operator could easily have pushed him aside. But a cable caught his foot and he fell sideways, knocking the man from his stool and clutching the apparatus to support himself.

Clutching the resistance control – twisting the knob over

to full power. Seeing the soft glow become a blinding, searing, three thousand candle-power ray – hearing a voice scream. But not a woman's scream – not the cry of a human being. The sound Harry heard was quite unearthly, because the creature that made it had come from the pit and was about to return there.

But just before Miss Vallance died and her face toppled against the white-hot carbons, Harry saw something that made him echo that scream. The eyes – the single eye – the gift that Krisia Bathori had begged Satan to pass on to her child – was turned in his direction.

# Postscript

'Don't worry Harry. The bullet concussed you briefly and your second blackout was due to delayed shock and loss of blood.' Miriam stood beside his bed in the hospital. 'But the skull was not penetrated and no cerebral damage has been done.' She looked at an X-ray slide. 'There's a fracture, of course, but only a minor one which will knit of its own accord, and you'll soon be as good as new.'

'I doubt that, Miriam.' Harry could still hear Miss Vallance's agonized cry and see her face toppling towards the lamp before his hand slipped from the switch and the world went dark. 'Nothing will ever be the same.'

'Quite true, my boy. You'll have a scar across your forehead for one thing.' John Forest was also in the room and he chuckled like a gurgling, partially-blocked drain. 'But that should prove no handicap. I've always heard that the fair sex find scars attractive, if they're romantically positioned.

'You're a fortunate fellow, Harry. A skull thick enough to deflect a bullet, applause and approbation and money in the offing – also luck. If you hadn't passed out after killing that woman, the stage hands would probably have lynched you. They may not have liked Susan Vallance, but you cost them their jobs.'

'I did kill her, didn't I?' Harry's mind was still numb and the past seemed much more real than the present. 'Miss Vallance is dead, but what about . . . ?'

'Her eyes?' Forest had had a long talk with Miriam and he finished the question. 'A rum thing that. The woman died of heart failure and her face was not badly burned, apart from one feature. She had no eyes. They had completely disintegrated and the sockets were empty.'

'The Moslems are right, then. The heat of the sun can defeat the force and a carbon arc had the same effect.' Harry saw that Forest was not the only man present. 'Hullo, Inspector Munro. I'm afraid I don't know whether I should wish you good day or good morning.'

'Morning would be the appropriate greeting, and it's exactly three minutes past midnight.' Munro had looked at his watch. 'Yes, as Mr Forest has said, you're a lucky chap, and not just because you're alive. We don't like people who take the law into their own hands, and even though those bodies in Miss Vallance's flat prove she was a murderess, the Public Prosecutor might have preferred charges against you.' The inspector was suffering from hay fever and his voice was almost as thick as Forest's. 'However, we have found a diary which shows that you were fully justified.

'Though I've only glanced through the contents briefly, Miss Vallance has recorded all her experiences, actions and intentions. Dreams which told her that she was a chosen instrument of destruction. A family history which persuaded her she could adopt the powers of Countess Bathori's niece. Her meeting with Trenton at a seance and the realization that they were kindred spirits. The robbery at Flethertarn Hall, the death of the thieves and the eye graft.' Munro blew his nose loudly. 'Finally her plans for this evening. If you hadn't intervened in the nick of time, the whole audience might have been infected like Starr and his confederates.'

'Gentlemen, I think you'd better leave now.' Miriam had been watching Harry intently. 'Mr Clay is very tired and he must get some sleep.'

'In a moment, my dear, but I'm sure he's not too tired to discuss money.' Forest produced a legal document from his briefcase. 'A lot of money and a lot of pleasant publicity, Harry, because in spite of the lateness of the hour I've been busy on the blower and the typewriter.

'This is a contract confirming that you've got your old job on the *Globe* back and you will be paid twelve thousand pounds to write the story for our weekly supplement. You will also have a percentage of the syndicated sales and retain all book, film and television rights. And those rights will be worth a packet, my boy. Can't you see the paperback cover and the cinema hoardings? "Evil Eyes at the Pegasus."

'Yes, perhaps that is a bit corny.' Harry had not responded and the fat man chuckled again. 'But have no fear. We'll dream up a catchy title in time, so try to look cheerful because you're on top of the world. Fame and lolly and public acclaim. Love too – judging by Dr Stanford's concern for your welfare.

'Though she damn near set me on fire, you've got a smashing girl there – a real cracker.' The archness was repellent, but it was not that which made Harry shudder and stare at Forest's shirt cuffs.

'Well, we must obey Doctor's orders, so just sign this contract and I'll leave you to have a bit of shut-eye.' Forest took a pen from his pocket and drew closer to the bed. 'Don't bother to check the details, because I drew up the schedule myself.'

'No – no, John. Don't come near me.' Harry was cowering against the pillows. 'Keep back – please don't come any nearer.'

'What on earth's the matter, son?' Forest was both surprised and offended. 'I said that I drew up the schedule personally and I'm a pal. The terms are extremely generous and you can trust your Uncle John to give you a square deal.'

'I don't want a deal. I don't care a damn about a contract.' Harry's voice was agonized. 'All I want is to be left alone, so look at your wrists, John . . . Look at your wrists.'

'Oh, you mean the dressings.' Forest glanced at the strips of sticking plaster covering his burns and then grinned waggishly at Miriam. 'Your lady friend was responsible for my injuries, but not to worry. The damage is only superficial and I'm not one to bear a grudge against attractive females.'

'Hands, you fool.' The words were barely audible. 'Hands – things on hands.'

'Sorry, Harry, I didn't get that, though I think I know what's bothering you. It's not my hands, but your own which present a problem. You feel too weak and shaky to hold the paper and sign your name.

'That difficulty is easily overcome, me old son.' Forest was eager to complete the deal and his tone was full of jocular reassurance. 'I'm familiar with your writing and I'll help you guide the pen. Who'll question a sprawled signature if it's witnessed by the inspector and Dr Stanford?'

'Are you blind, John? Have you lost all sense of touch and feeling?' Harry whimpered as Forest leaned over him. 'Stop them, Miriam. For the love of God – stop them.'

'Nothing is going to harm you, darling, and you must keep calm.' Miriam spoke soothingly, but she suspected what might have happened and her anxieties were rising. 'Please stand back from the bed, Mr Forest. Harry is in no condition to think about business.

'Stand back, I say.' The order was rapped out, Forest obeyed, but Harry saw that Miriam had delivered it too late. There could be no escape for him because the door of Room One Hundred and One was open.

Just before Susan Vallance died he had looked her full in the face and nobody could protect him from the things that had emerged from the sleeves of Forest's shirt, crawled across Forest's thick wrists and stubby fingers and dropped on to the bed. Small, lithe, hideous things wriggling purposefully up the sheet towards his ears. The worst things in the world.

# RECENT AND FORTHCOMING TITLES FROM VALANCOURT BOOKS

| | |
|---|---|
| Michael Arlen | Hell! said the Duchess |
| R. C. Ashby | He Arrived at Dusk |
| Frank Baker | The Birds |
| Walter Baxter | Look Down in Mercy |
| Charles Beaumont | The Hunger and Other Stories |
| David Benedictus | The Fourth of June |
| Paul Binding | Harmonica's Bridegroom |
| Charles Birkin | The Smell of Evil |
| John Blackburn | A Scent of New-Mown Hay |
| | Broken Boy |
| | Blue Octavo |
| | A Ring of Roses |
| | Children of the Night |
| | The Flame and the Wind |
| | Nothing but the Night |
| | Bury Him Darkly |
| | The Household Traitors |
| | The Face of the Lion |
| | The Cyclops Goblet |
| | A Beastly Business |
| Thomas Blackburn | A Clip of Steel |
| | The Feast of the Wolf |
| Michael Blumlein | The Brains of Rats |
| John Braine | Room at the Top |
| | The Vodi |
| | Life at the Top |
| Michael Campbell | Lord Dismiss Us |
| Basil Copper | The Great White Space |
| | Necropolis |
| | The House of the Wolf |
| Hunter Davies | Body Charge |
| Jennifer Dawson | The Ha-Ha |
| A. E. Ellis | The Rack |
| Barry England | Figures in a Landscape |
| Ronald Fraser | Flower Phantoms |
| Michael Frayn | The Tin Men |
| | The Russian Interpreter |
| | Towards the End of the Morning |
| | A Very Private Life |
| | Sweet Dreams |

| | |
|---|---|
| Gillian Freeman | The Liberty Man |
| | The Leather Boys |
| | The Leader |
| Rodney Garland | The Heart in Exile |
| Stephen Gilbert | The Landslide |
| | Monkeyface |
| | The Burnaby Experiments |
| | Ratman's Notebooks |
| Martyn Goff | The Plaster Fabric |
| | The Youngest Director |
| Stephen Gregory | The Cormorant |
| | The Woodwitch |
| | The Blood of Angels |
| Alex Hamilton | Beam of Malice |
| Thomas Hinde | The Day the Call Came |
| Claude Houghton | Neighbours |
| | I Am Jonathan Scrivener |
| | This Was Ivor Trent |
| Fred Hoyle | The Black Cloud |
| Alan Judd | The Devil's Own Work |
| James Kennaway | The Mind Benders |
| | The Cost of Living Like This |
| Gerald Kersh | Fowlers End |
| | Nightshade and Damnations |
| | Clock Without Hands |
| | Neither Man Nor Dog |
| | On an Odd Note |
| Francis King | To the Dark Tower |
| | Never Again |
| | An Air That Kills |
| | The Dividing Stream |
| | The Dark Glasses |
| | The Man on the Rock |
| C.H.B. Kitchin | The Sensitive One |
| | Birthday Party |
| | Ten Pollitt Place |
| | The Book of Life |
| | A Short Walk in Williams Park |
| Hilda Lewis | The Witch and the Priest |
| John Lodwick | Brother Death |
| Kenneth Martin | Aubade |
| Michael McDowell | The Amulet |
| | The Elementals |

| | |
|---|---|
| Michael Nelson | Knock or Ring |
| | A Room in Chelsea Square |
| Beverley Nichols | Crazy Pavements |
| Oliver Onions | The Hand of Kornelius Voyt |
| Christopher Priest | The Affirmation |
| J.B. Priestley | Benighted |
| | The Doomsday Men |
| | The Other Place |
| | The Magicians |
| | Saturn Over the Water |
| | The Shapes of Sleep |
| | The Thirty-First of June |
| | Salt Is Leaving |
| Peter Prince | Play Things |
| Piers Paul Read | Monk Dawson |
| Forrest Reid | Brian Westby |
| | The Tom Barber Trilogy |
| | Denis Bracknel |
| Andrew Sinclair | The Raker |
| | Gog |
| | The Facts in the Case of E. A. Poe |
| David Storey | Radcliffe |
| | Pasmore |
| | Saville |
| Bernard Taylor | The Godsend |
| | Sweetheart, Sweetheart |
| Russell Thorndike | The Slype |
| | The Master of the Macabre |
| John Wain | Hurry on Down |
| | Strike the Father Dead |
| | The Smaller Sky |
| | A Winter in the Hills |
| Hugh Walpole | The Killer and the Slain |
| Keith Waterhouse | There is a Happy Land |
| | Billy Liar |
| | Jubb |
| | Billy Liar on the Moon |
| Colin Wilson | Ritual in the Dark |
| | Man Without a Shadow |
| | The World of Violence |
| | Necessary Doubt |
| | The Glass Cage |
| | The Philosopher's Stone |
| | The God of the Labyrinth |